"I *trusted* you!"

"I don't think trust played that big a role in your decision to marry me," Alex countered very dryly.

"Of course it did!"

"No, Sara. Your objective was to marry well and save face. I do believe I'm the male equivalent of a trophy wife in so far as you actually take notice of my existence. So don't accuse me of using you, *cara*.... As I see it, I'm the one who's allowed himself to be used."

'Look at me....' Alex demanded.

LYNNE GRAHAM was born in Northern Ireland and has been a keen romance reader since her teens. She is very happily married, with an understanding husband, who has learned to cook since she started to write! Her three children, two of whom are adopted, keep her on her toes. She also has a very large wolfhound, who knocks over everything with her tail, and an even more-adored mongrel, who rules everybody. When time allows, Lynne is a keen gardener and loves experimenting with Italian cookery.

Books by Lynne Graham

HARLEQUIN PRESENTS
1551—TEMPESTUOUS REUNION
1696—A VENGEFUL PASSION
1712—ANGEL OF DARKNESS
1758—BOND OF HATRED
1779—THE UNFAITHFUL WIFE
1792—CRIME OF PASSION
1824—A SAVAGE BETRAYAL

LYNNE GRAHAM

The Trophy Husband

Harlequin Books

TORONTO • NEW YORK • LONDON
AMSTERDAM • PARIS • SYDNEY • HAMBURG
STOCKHOLM • ATHENS • TOKYO • MILAN
MADRID • WARSAW • BUDAPEST • AUCKLAND

ISBN 0-373-11835-X

THE TROPHY HUSBAND

First North American Publication 1996.

CHAPTER ONE

SARA paid off the taxi in a breathless rush and raced up the stairs to the flat she shared with Antonia. Had they been burgled? Had someone in the family had an accident? Worse still, had something happened to Brian? Her imagination had gone into overdrive since she had received Antonia's message at work.

'Miss Dalton said you had to come home immediately, that it was very urgent,' the girl on the switchboard had stressed anxiously. 'I hope it isn't bad news, Miss Lacey. She wouldn't even wait for me to put her call through.'

Crossing the landing at speed, Sara unlocked the door of the flat. It was a disorientating experience. Loud music assaulted her ears. Phil Collins' latest album was playing full blast. A single electric-blue court shoe lay abandoned like a question mark on the hall carpet.

'Antonia?' Sara called, a quick frown of bewilderment drawing her fine brows together as she glanced into the empty lounge. The bedroom door was ajar. She pressed it back.

'Antonia?' she said again, and only then did she see the half-naked couple passionately entangled on the rumpled bed.

'*Sara*?' her cousin squealed as she reeled up, her honey-blonde hair wildly mussed up, her pink mouth swollen, pale blue eyes wide with horror.

In the very act of embarrassed retreat, Sara froze. Her attention had lodged on the tousled male head lifting off the white pillows. Recognition hit her like a punch in the stomach. Cruel fingers clutched at her heart and her lungs, tripping her heartbeat, depriving her of the air she needed to breathe.

5

'Oh, my God...' Brian groaned, grabbing up his shirt and rolling off the bed in one appalled movement.

Antonia was frantically struggling back into her blouse. 'Why the hell aren't you at work?' she screamed.

'You phoned...left a message that I was to come home,' Sara framed unevenly, not even recognising the distant voice that emerged from her bloodless lips as her own.

'*I* phoned? Are you crazy?' Antonia shrieked furiously. 'Whoever phoned, you can be sure it wasn't me!'

'You bitch, Toni!' Brian bit out in stricken condemnation. 'You deliberately set me up—'

'Don't be stupid!' Antonia hissed, but then without warning defiance replaced her angry discomfiture. She rested malicious blue eyes on Sara, who was already backing away on legs that were threatening to fold beneath her. 'But I did warn you that Brian was mine for the asking...didn't I?'

'No...' Brian's voice wavered weakly as his gaze collided with Sara's shattered green eyes—pools of stark pain in the dead white stillness of her triangular face. He made a sudden move towards her, both hands raised and extended as if to draw her back to him. 'This has never happened before, Sara...I *swear* it!'

Sara turned jerkily away and fled. She nearly fell down the last flight of stairs—Brian's frantic calls from the landing above acted on her like a trip-wire. Blocking him out, she steadied herself with one shaking hand on the dingy wall and made herself breathe in slowly and deeply before she walked back out onto the street.

Antonia and Brian. Brian and Antonia. She stared down numbly at the ring on her engagement finger. Her stomach lurched in violent protest. Six weeks off the wedding day...her cousin and her fiancé. It was as if the world had stopped turning suddenly, flinging her off into frightening free fall. She was in shock—so deep in shock that she couldn't even think. But her memory was relentlessly throwing up scraps of dialogue from the recent past.

'Brian chose you like he chooses his shirts...you've got to look good at the company dinners and wear a long time!' Antonia had sniped.

'Three years ago I could have lifted one little finger and Brian would have come running... He really had it bad for me.' Antonia had savoured the words.

Sara squared her narrow shoulders, caught a glimpse of herself in a shop window and stared. She saw a small woman with black hair worn in a tidy French plait, dressed in an unexciting navy business suit and white blouse. No competition for a five-foot-ten-inch blonde who had once made it between the covers of *Vogue*. She felt as if she was dying inside. She didn't know what to do, where to go.

A bus was drawing up at the stop several yards away and she started to run. Her dazed eyes skimmed over the man standing in a nearby doorway. He turned his head abruptly, making her wonder if she looked as odd as she felt. She didn't notice that the man swiftly fell into step behind her and climbed on the same bus.

'Do we have to have Antonia as a bridesmaid? My mother can't stand her,' Brian had complained peevishly.

'She's a real tart,' he had muttered with distaste. 'No decent woman would take her clothes off for money...'

Still with the same man tracking patiently in her wake, but quite unaware of his presence, Sara wandered back into the hugely impressive London headquarters of Rossini Industries. When the receptionist on the penultimate floor addressed her, Sara didn't hear her. Blind and deaf, she was moving on automatic pilot. She entered the spacious office which she shared with Pete Hunniford. It was empty. Pete's wife had gone into labour mid-morning, she recalled then. It was like remembering something that had happened a lifetime ago.

Her phone was buzzing like an angry wasp. She sat down and answered it.

'Tasmin Laslo here. I want to speak to Alex,' a taut female voice demanded.

'Mr Rossini is in conference. I am so sorry. Would you like me to—?'

The actress said a very rude word. 'You're lying, aren't you?'

Sara had been lying to Alex Rossini's women for the entire year that she had been employed as his social secretary. Alex Rossini was very rarely available to his lovers during office hours, and when a name was removed from a certain regularly updated list he was never available again. Lying went with the territory, no matter how much Sara despised the necessity.

'He sent me a diamond bracelet while I was filming in Hungary and I knew it was over!' Tasmin suddenly spat tempestuously. 'He's found someone else, hasn't he?'

'You're better off without him, Miss Laslo,' Sara heard herself saying. 'You're a wonderful actress. You're wasted on a slick, womanising swine like Alex Rossini!'

Incredulous silence hummed on the line. 'I beg your pardon?' Tasmin finally gasped.

Sara looked down dazedly at the receiver and thrust it back on the cradle in shock. She was trembling all over. Dear heaven, had she really said that? She rose unsteadily upright again. Her stomach cramped with sudden, unbearable nausea. She lurched into the cloakroom across the corridor and was horribly sick.

Ten minutes later, still shaking like a leaf, she returned to her office. The phone was buzzing again. She ignored it, walked over to Pete's desk and withdrew the bottle of brandy that he kept in the bottom drawer. She poured a liberal amount into a cup and slowly drank it down, grimacing at the unfamiliar taste of alcohol. Maybe it would settle her stomach. Brian and Antonia. Their names linked in a ceaseless refrain inside her pounding head, making her want to smash her head against the wall in protest.

She felt as if she was going mad. Sensible, steady Sara, who always kept her head in a crisis. But Sara had never before faced a crisis in which her whole world had fallen apart. Shivering, she helped herself to another nip of brandy, struggling to get a grip on herself. 'No decent woman...' A choked and humourless laugh escaped her. She tore the ring off her finger, dropped it in a drawer and rammed the drawer shut. She made herself pick up the phone again.

Unfortunately it was her aunt on the line. Something about the wedding rehearsal. Sara froze while Antonia's mother talked. Then she sat down, and drew in a deep, shuddering breath. 'Aunt Janice?' She hesitated and then forced herself on. 'I'm sorry but the wedding's off. Brian and I have broken up.' Even to her own ears she sounded unreal, like someone clumsily cracking a joke in the worst possible taste.

'Don't be silly, Sara,' Janice Dalton murmured sharply. 'What on earth are you talking about?'

'Brian and I have broken up. I'm very sorry... but we've decided we can't get married after all.'

'If you've had some foolish argument with Brian, I suggest you sort it out quickly,' her aunt told her with icy restraint. 'Brian had lunch with us yesterday and there was nothing wrong then!'

The line went dead as her aunt cut the connection. Sara trembled. Antonia's mother... how could she have told her the truth? Janice and Hugh Dalton had given her a home when her own mother had died. How could she possibly tell them the truth? Much better simply to pretend that she and Brian had had a change of heart— much cleaner, much less embarrassing for all concerned. The two families were neighbours and friends. A giant lump thickened her throat. Did Brian *love* Antonia?

'No decent woman...' Antonia had shed her clothes with alacrity when she had been offered the chance to feature in the famous Rossini calendar. Marco, Alex Rossini's kid brother, had smoothly offered Sara the same opportunity, unperturbed by her incredulous embarrassment. 'You've got something your long, tall cousin hasn't got... You're really sexy... and you have a lot of class.'

Marco had made the invitation in front of a highly amused audience at the staff party and it had become a tormenting, running joke in the months which had followed. The instant that Marco had seen Sara redden he had realised that he had found a real live target. Every time he saw Sara, he offered her an increasingly fantastic sum to bare all. No doubt he saw in her what everyone wanted to see, Sara reflected bitterly: a woman the exact, boring opposite of her exciting, beautiful cousin. Prim, quiet, predictable, ludicrously unlikely ever to set the world... or indeed any man... on fire.

Antonia had had Sara christened Prissy Prude at school, and, having created that image for her, had then delighted in shattering it by sharing the news that Sara was illegitimate, the inconvenient result of her youthful mother's holiday fling with a Greek waiter. Some of the girls hadn't laughed at first but they had soon fallen into line and obediently giggled and sneered. After all, Antonia had been the undeniable leader of the pack and peer pressure had been relentless. Sara had duly been persecuted, no other girl daring to stand her ground against Antonia lest she find herself enduring the same ordeal. To escape, Sara had left school at sixteen and taken a secretarial course. And that had not been her dream.

But Brian *had* been her dream...

Suddenly, with a violence that shook her, Sara hated everything about herself—her body, her personality, her inhibitions, her clothing. She *was* boring, laughably out of step with other women in her age group. Old-fashioned, sexually ignorant, eager to give up her job and become a housewife and mother at twenty-three. She should have been born a century ago, not in the nineties.

Out of the corner of her eye, she finally noticed that the door was open. Slowly she lifted her head and panic filled her, her cat-green eyes flying wide to accentuate the exotic slant of her cheekbones. Alex Rossini was standing there as silent as a sleek predator on the prowl . . . and both phones were ringing off the hook, unanswered. He should have been in Rome this afternoon, not here in London, she thought stupidly.

'Coffee-break?' Alex murmured in a curiously quiet voice instead of letting fly at her as she had expected. The phones stopped abruptly as if the switchboard had cut them off, plunging them into a sudden, thunderous silence.

In a daze, she looked back at him. Six feet three inches of lithe, rawly virile masculinity. Black hair, hard bronze profile with the deep, dark, flashing eyes of his Italian ancestry. A sexually devastating male with an over-whelmingly physical presence that few men could equal. And Sara hated being near him. She hated the way he looked at her. She hated the way he spoke to her.

If the cost of setting up the first marital home hadn't been so extortionate, Sara would have sacrificed her excellent salary and taken a lesser position elsewhere within a week of being exposed to Alex Rossini's sardonic asides and contemptuously amused appraisals. He made her feel so murderously uncomfortable . . . so self-conscious, so *ridiculous*. He made her feel like a curious specimen trapped behind museum glass.

'Finish your coffee.' A lean, long-fingered brown hand casually closed round the half-full cup of brandy sitting on the edge of her desk and extended it to her.

Didn't he smell the alcohol, realise that it wasn't black coffee? Evidently, obviously not. Jerkily, she reached out and accepted the cup and focused on his beautifully polished shoes, every muscle whip-taut. She tossed back the rest of the brandy in a burning surge. It brought tears to her eyes, which she blinked back furiously.

'Where's Pete?'

'Still at the hospital with his wife.' Sara struggled for some desperate semblance of normality, astonished that he wasn't cutting her to ribbons with the satirical edge of his tongue. She forced herself upright, bracing both hands on the desk. Involuntarily her gaze collided with shimmering dark golden eyes and it was like falling on an electric fence, shock waves making every raw nerve-ending scream. Deliberately she turned her head away, closing him out again. No, she was not susceptible. She had proved that to her satisfaction over and over again.

'Then I'm afraid you'll have to take his place.'

'His place?' Nobody could possibly take Pete Hunniford's place. Pete was Alex's most devoted gofer. Nothing came between Pete and ambition. He had freely admitted to Sara that his first marriage had fallen apart because he was never at home. And right at this minute, if Alex employed his mobile phone, Pete would be out of the labour ward like a rocket.

'Nothing too onerous... *Relax,*' Alex breathed in that distinctively rich dark voice which rolled down her spine like golden honey, burning wherever it touched. 'I only want you to take down a couple of letters.'

Her brow furrowed as she automatically lifted a pad and pencils. He was talking very slowly, not with his usual quick impatience. He hadn't even asked her why she hadn't answered the phones. He stood back for her to precede him from the room, and in her need to keep as much physical space between them as possible she jerked sideways and skidded off balance.

Strong hands whipped out and closed round her upper arms to steady her. Her head swam, her heartbeat kicking wildly against her breastbone. She quivered, fighting off sudden dizziness, and he drew her back. 'OK?' he murmured, still holding her on the threshold.

'F-fine... Sorry.' Her nostrils flared in dismay as the warm, definably male scent of him washed over her. Aromatic, intrinsically familiar... intimate. *Intimate*? What was the matter with her? What the heck was the matter with her? As she stiffened he released her and she walked down the corridor with careful small steps, noticing that the double doors of his office at the end looked peculiarly out of focus. Now near, now far, now skewed. All that brandy. Drunk in charge of a phone. But it felt shamelessly, unbelievably good: a short-term anaesthetic against the enormous pain waiting to jump on her—the pain she could not yet face head-on. As long as she didn't think, she could protect herself.

'Sit down, Sara.' She plotted a course across the thick carpet with immense care and sank down on the nearest seat, suddenly terrified that he would notice the state she was in. Being intoxicated suddenly didn't feel good any more. In Alex Rossini's presence, it felt like sheer insanity. Discovery would be unbelievably demeaning.

Disorientatedly, she glanced up and found him standing over her. She flinched. Her hands trembled and she anchored them tightly round the pad. He didn't sit down. He strolled with silent grace across to the floor-length windows. A stunningly handsome man, he had an innate elegance of movement, his superbly cut mohair and silk-blend charcoal-grey suit the perfect complementary frame to wide shoulders, lean hips and long, powerful thighs.

From beneath luxuriant black lashes he surveyed her. 'Shall I begin?'

He didn't normally request permission. Uncertainly she nodded. He dictated with incredibly long pauses that enabled her more or less to keep up but she still missed bits because her mind wouldn't stay in one place. Shock was giving way to reality, denial giving way to bursts of agonised pain. For how long had Brian been deceiving her with Antonia? Her memory threw up the image of the open bottle of wine in the lounge, the half-filled wineglasses by the bed. No sudden passion there. They had carried the glasses with them into the bedroom. A carefully staged lunchtime encounter when Sara should have been at work.

'Did you get all that?'

The page currently beneath her fingers was blank. Briefly she simply closed her eyes, willing herself to find calm and control.

'It's all right, Sara... the letter isn't important.'

The softness of the assurance astonished her. Dazedly she glanced up, encountered Alex Rossini's brilliant dark eyes and was mesmerised by the sincerity she read there. He was resting against the edge of his polished desk, far too close for comfort. He reached down and removed the pad from her nerveless fingers, setting it carelessly aside.

'Something has upset you...' he drawled.

Her creamy, perfect skin tightened over her fine facial bones as she focused on his silk tie. 'No...'

'You're not wearing your ring.'

Sara went white. The pencil she was fiddling with snapped in two.

'You are clearly distressed,' Alex murmured in the same quiet, disturbingly gentle tone which she had never heard him employ before. 'I believe you were called home unexpectedly this morning. What happened there?'

She was appalled to discover that she wanted to tell him, spill out the poison building up inside her, but instead she bit down hard on her tongue.

'Perhaps you would prefer to go home for the rest of the day?' Alex suggested lethally.

'No...' Sara muttered, horror bringing her back to life. Antonia would be waiting for her and she could not yet face that confrontation.

'Why not?' he prompted her.

'I found my fiancé in bed with my cousin.' As soon as she had said it she could not believe that she had said *that* out loud and to him of all people. A tide of chagrined colour crawled up her slender throat.

But Alex Rossini didn't bat a magnificent eyelash and his response was instantaneous. 'A merciful escape.'

'Escape?' Sara queried blankly.

Alex spread beautifully shaped brown hands expressively. 'Think how much more disturbing it would have been had you discovered such a sordid liaison *after* the wedding.'

'There isn't going to be a wedding now,' Sara said shakily, and whereas telling that same fact to her aunt had seemed like part of a living nightmare it now felt like hard, agonising reality.

'Of course not. No woman would forgive such a betrayal, would she?' Alex drawled softly.

The silence hummed. The tip of her tongue snaked out to moisten her dry lower lip. Forgiveness... understanding. Brian had been asking for both within seconds. He had not stood shoulder to shoulder with Antonia...

'After all,' Alex continued with honeyed persistence. 'How could you ever trust him again? Or her?'

The darkness sank back down over Sara where for an instant she had seen a wild, hopeful chink of light.

'Were you thinking of giving him another chance?' Alex enquired in a tone of polite astonishment.

Sara flinched. 'No,' she muttered sickly, duly forced to see the impossibility of ever trusting again.

Yet she could not believe that she was actually having such a conversation with Alex Rossini, who was not known for his concerned and benevolent interest in his employees' personal problems. Indeed, the Rossini credo was that the best employees left their private life outside the door of Rossini Industries and never, ever allowed that private life to interfere with their work.

'Why are you talking to me like this?' she whispered helplessly.

'Do you have anyone else to confide in?'

Sara tried and failed to swallow. It was almost as if he knew, but how could he possibly *know* how frighteningly isolated she now was? She could not turn to Antonia's parents and she had no other relatives, no close friends who were not also Brian's friends or colleagues. 'No, but—'

'Nothing you have told me will go any further,' Alex asserted, his night-dark eyes, sharp and shrewd as knives, trained on her, but those eyes were no longer cutting, no longer cold, no longer grimly amused.

'You're being so...so kind,' Sara said in a wobbly tone as she fought to conceal her disbelief, for this was a side of his character that she had never thought to see, indeed never dreamt existed.

'You have had a traumatic experience and, naturally, I am concerned.'

'Thank you, but I don't need your pity,' Sara bit out painfully.

'The very last thing you inspire is pity,' Alex assured her, unleashing a wry smile of reproof on her. 'You should be celebrating your freedom. Life is far too short for regrets. You've already wasted two years of it on that little salesman. The future has to offer far more entertaining possibilities—'

'How did you know Brian was a salesman?' Sara breathed, the words slurring slightly.

'Isn't he? He looks like one,' Alex informed her smoothly.

Something not quite right tugged at her instincts and then drifted away again, for nothing in her entire world was right any more.

'You live with your cousin, don't you?' Alex probed.

Again she was disconcerted by his knowledge and perhaps it showed, because he added, 'Marco mentioned it to me.'

'Yes.' Sara flushed, reluctantly recalling all the unwanted, gory details which had been forced on her during Antonia's short-lived affair with Alex's brother. That connection had embarrassed Sara.

'Naturally you do not want to return to your home at this moment,' Alex murmured, and casually tossed a set of keys onto her lap. 'You can use the company apartment until you have made other arrangements.'

Even in the state she was in Sara was staggered by such a proposition. The apartment was a penthouse on the floor above, used only by the Rossini family and, very occasionally, their personal friends. 'I couldn't possibly—'

'Where else have you got to go?'

She clutched the keys, meaning to return them but thinking helplessly of the humiliation of dealing with Antonia as she felt now. Her strained eyes unguarded and vulnerable, Sara stared back at him. 'I'm very grateful.'

'A fresh start,' Alex murmured intently. 'I'm having a dinner party tonight. Why don't you come? You shouldn't be on your own.'

A nervous laugh lodged in her aching throat. *A party?* He thought that she was in the mood for a party? Was he insane or just downright incapable of comprehending the immensity of what had happened to her today?

'I'll be fine,' she returned tremulously, wondering if he needed someone to supervise the caterers. Pete usually attended Alex's dinner parties, checked the seating arrangements, oiled the conversation and ensured that everything went smoothly. Alex Rossini paid for that kind of service. Alex Rossini was so rich that he could afford to burn money for amusement.

'I'll call you later. I'll send a car to pick you up at seven,' Alex told her as if she hadn't spoken.

Dully she fumbled for an excuse. 'I have nothing—'

'I'll buy you a dress to wear. No problem, *cara*. Don't even think about something so trivial.'

'But I—'

Strong brown hands reached down and closed over hers, tugging her gently upright. He angled her towards the door as if she were a walking doll. 'Go up to the apartment and lie down for a while; practise thinking optimistic, happy thoughts. Smile...' he urged

softly, and a blunt fingertip skimmed below the trembling curve of her full lower lip and withdrew again, the
contact feather-light and strangely soothing.

Unwarily, like someone in a dream, Sara looked up
at him, connected with shimmering, mesmeric gold eyes
and staggered slightly. He balanced her again with ease.
An ache unlike anything she had ever experienced made
her shiver. 'Mr Rossini—'

'Alex ... *Cristo*!' he exploded, abruptly freeing her.

Sara almost fell over. Numbly she watched him stride
over to sweep up the phone that she hadn't even heard
ringing. He swung smoothly back to her. 'Go up to the
apartment and lie down,' he instructed her again.

Sara backed out slowly and walked back down to her
office to collect her bag. Her head was aching. She put
a hand up to her hair and undid the tight plait, running
her fingers through the loosened tresses. The phone on
her desk was ringing. For an instant she hesitated, and
then she lifted it.

'Sara?' Pete demanded impatiently. 'Where have you
been?'

'I was—'

'Look, I need a favour,' he broke in. 'Alex told me
to get Marco's signature on some papers yesterday but
I forgot. They're in the top right-hand drawer in my desk.
Take a cab over to the studio and get it seen to before
Alex asks for them ... OK?'

Sara took a deep breath, grimaced and then wearily
sighed. 'OK.'

'You're an angel. I bet your replacement won't be half
so helpful.'

The reminder that she was actually working out her
notice hit Sara hard as she climbed into a taxi. She would
be in the dole queue soon, she realised dully. Her suc-
cessor was already picked, due to take her place in a
fortnight's time. Brian hadn't wanted a working wife.
And she had no savings. She had poured every penny
of her salary into renovating and furnishing the Victorian

terrace house that Brian had bought. Weekends and evenings, she had scraped walls, plastered, decorated, cut out and sewn and hung curtains. She had put her heart into transforming that house. The knowledge that now she would never live there sank in on her slowly and then blistered her soul like an acid burn.

Real anger began to rise inside her. Three years ago Sara had stood by, watching Brian pursue Antonia without success. But her cousin would take just for the sake of taking, and throughout the years that Sara had lived in the Dalton home she had been taught that lesson over and over again. Anything she had been foolish enough to value had inevitably been taken from her by her cousin... only this time it had not been a toy or a sentimental keepsake, it had been the man she loved. She clambered dizzily out of the cab with a white, frozen face.

She had never been in Marco Rossini's high-tech photographic studio before. The reception area was incredibly busy. It made her feel claustrophobic. She forced her passage through the throng and trekked down the corridor indicated by the laconic redhead on the desk.

Marco was lying back in a chair inside the perimeter of a blinding circle of lights in an empty studio. He looked half-asleep but his mobile dark brows hit his hairline at speed when he saw Sara hovering, and he sprang upright with a mocking smile. 'To what do I owe the honour? Don't tell me you've finally decided to take me up on my offer? Miss December in red boots and a tasteful sprinkling of holly berries...what do you think?'

Sara gritted her teeth as she felt her cheeks burn. She was in no mood to take one of Marco's baiting sessions. Evading his malicious gaze, she murmured flatly as she extended the file, 'These documents require your signature.'

Marco suddenly laughed.

'What's so funny?' Sara heard herself demand almost aggressively, the words slurring slightly.

'Private joke.'

'If it's about me, it's not private!' Sara told him fiercely, standing her ground.

Marco surveyed her with intense amusement. 'There's a price.'

'A price?'

Marco laughed again. 'You tell me something first...haven't you ever once got the hots in my brother's radius?'

Sara looked back at him blankly. 'Excuse me?'

'Alex is a very good-looking guy, beats the women off with sticks. If he wasn't family, I'd hate the smooth bastard! Come on, you can tell me...if it wasn't for true love, you'd have given him a whirl, right? You know that movie where Robert Redford pays a million bucks for one night with Demi Moore—*Indecent Proposal*? You too could have made your fortune...'

'I don't understand.' It was a lie. Sara just couldn't believe what Marco was insinuating.

Marco dealt her an incredulous glance. 'Are you saying you didn't even notice? Or are you telling me that Alex didn't once chance his arm?'

'If you are trying to imply that your brother is attracted to me, you're wrong—'

'To the tune of a million bucks? He could drop a million without noticing. No, the sum I heard mentioned was two million,' Marco imparted with undeniable relish. 'I think Alex thought just one was bargain basement.'

Sara's head was swimming again. It was so hot beneath the lights that she couldn't concentrate. 'This is a very distasteful conversation, Marco.'

'So Alex wants to jump your bones...is that some sort of crime? Lust makes the world go round,' he told her impatiently.

Alex Rossini wanted to go to bed with her? Her lashes fluttered in bemusement. She couldn't believe it.

Marco shook his head slowly. 'You really didn't know, did you? Love is truly blind. But hey, don't let your heart soften in his direction. Remind yourself that you don't like him and steer clear. Marry your insurance salesman and live happily ever after,' he advised very drily as he flipped through the file and began scrawling his signature.

Alex Rossini *wanted* her? Rubbish, nonsense, Marco's deliberate mistake—doubtless another example of his nasty sense of humour. 'You don't like him'. Had her dislike of Alex Rossini been so obvious that even his brother was aware of it? She remembered Alex's astonishing kindness and tolerance and a stark arrow of guilt abruptly pierced her.

No, she had never liked Alex Rossini—his arrogance, his impatience, his sardonic tongue, his rich man's self-centred motivation which took no account of anything but his own wishes, his own needs. She had never liked the way he treated women either. As if they were *things* that he could buy and discard when he got bored... and he got bored so fast that your head would spin. Fast cars, fast women, fast-lane life. Nightclubs, movie premières, gambling joints, summer in the South of France, winter in the Alps. When the beautiful face and body of his latest lover palled, she got twenty-four regulation red roses and a diamond bracelet. Imaginative in that line he wasn't.

Why should he be? Women were easy around Alex Rossini. *He* didn't need to lie and cheat and deceive. *He* had no need to make promises that he had no intention of keeping...

Oh, Brian, how could you do this to me?

For the first time Sara met her own anguish head-on, and she swayed slightly, her temples pounding. The heat was suffocating her. Her blouse was sticking to her skin. In a clumsy movement she tugged off her jacket and breathed in deeply. Two million pounds... She wanted to laugh like a hysteric. It was so ridiculous...

'You know getting married costs a lot,' Marco murmured reflectively, watching Sara with fascinated eyes as the jacket slid from her limp fingers to the floor. 'Why don't you reconsider my offer? Nobody need ever know. I wouldn't be planning on publishing the shots. It could be your secret . . . and mine.'

As Sara attempted to focus on him, there was a sudden commotion out beyond the lights. A raw burst of Italian scorched her eardrums. A fist hit Marco on the shoulder, hard enough to knock him back, and suddenly Alex was there, ranting at his brother and with every blistering sentence punching him on the shoulder again, forcing him into retreat, like a boxer playing with a weak opponent.

White-faced, Marco leapt behind Sara. '*Dio* . . . switch him off before he kills somebody!'

CHAPTER TWO

SARA'S emerald-green eyes were wide with shock and incomprehension.

'I'm ashamed of you!' Alex roared at Marco, his strong features a mask of dark fury. 'For a bet, for a lousy fifty K. She's smashed out of her mind! She doesn't even know what day it is!'

'She's still a hell of a lot safer with me than she is with you!' Marco condemned furiously. 'And why shouldn't I have asked her?'

'Get out of my sight, you little jerk! Think yourself lucky it didn't go one step further—'

'All I did was make her an offer!' Marco shouted back.

'Then why's she got her jacket off?' Alex demanded with clenched fists.

'She took it off herself! Big deal! She wears more bloody clothes than Scott did in the Antarctic! Can nobody take a joke around here? I'm sorry, Sara,' Marco breathed harshly, turning back to her. 'I didn't know about your engagement, but now the deck is clear I would go for that two million and not a penny less!'

Shoulders unbowed, Marco walked away out beyond the lights.

'What the hell did you think you were doing coming over here in the state you're in?' Alex demanded with ferocious bite.

It was *her* turn, Sara registered numbly.

'Didn't I tell you to go and lie down? You could have fallen under a bus or something! When I realised you'd gone out again, I couldn't believe it!' Alex gritted, perfect white teeth flashing against sun-bronzed skin.

'I n-needed his signature on some papers.'

'So why did you take your jacket off?' Alex persisted.

23

'I was hot,' she muttered heavily.

Alex swept down a lean, impatient hand and lifted the article. '*Dio* . . . I should've worked that out for myself. A woman who wears her skirts below the knee and covers up every inch even in the heat of midsummer is highly unlikely to strip off for the camera. You're too much of a prude.'

Sara went suddenly rigid. Anger roared up through her without warning. 'I am *not* a prude!'

Alex had fallen very still. 'So you do have a temper,' he murmured in a tone of discovery.

'Just don't put me down,' she warned him unevenly, shaken now by the anger that had mushroomed up inside her and demanded an exit.

Alex drew fluidly back several paces and spread graceful brown hands. 'I was worried about you. You see, my creepy little brother laid a bet with me six months ago—'

'A bet?' Sara echoed with a frown.

'He bet me fifty thousand pounds that he could get you to pose in the nude.'

Sara shuddered, sick mortification flooding her.

'It never occurred to me that there was the slightest possibility you would fulfil that bet. You're not the type. It was a joke, Sara. Marco loves a good joke; sometimes, like today, he's tempted to take it too far.'

Sara studied the floor with burning eyes. She could feel the tears but they were mercifully dammed up. 'A good joke'. Her stomach twisted. A lousy male bet had lain behind Marco's constant baiting. A choked laugh fell from her tremulous mouth. She couldn't meet Alex's gaze. Marco had never had the smallest hope of winning his puerile bet but Alex had still chased after her. Why? Alex was already painfully well aware that she had gone off the rails once today. All along, she registered in anguished embarrassment, he had known that she was drunk.

'I've made an ass of myself,' she whispered with stinging bitterness.

'You *haven't* made an ass of yourself,' Alex breathed with raw emphasis. 'You've had a rough day. That's all.'

She quivered, a turmoil of emotion sweeping over her. She wanted Brian's arms round her so badly that she thought she would break apart. But Brian would never put his arms round her again. That was finished, dead, destroyed. More pain than she would have believed possible was suddenly coming at her from all sides. Her hands knotted together.

'You really love that bastard,' Alex murmured flatly.

She covered her cold face with spread fingers, as if she could somehow hold in what she was feeling. She fought to get a grip on herself again.

A pair of determined hands drew her forward and balanced her. With enormous effort, she managed to slide her arms obediently into the jacket which Alex extended.

'What was the crack about the two million?'

Sara's slender length tensed as she shakily tugged her hair out from beneath the collar of her jacket and shook it back out of her way.

'You have the most beautiful hair. I always wanted to see it loose.' Alex's dark eyes rested on the silky black torrent tumbling down to her waist. 'Don't ever get it cut.'

She slowly lifted her head, bewildered green eyes colliding with smouldering gold. It was electrifying. Stunned, she kept on looking at him. 'Marco said...Marco said you'd pay two million pounds for one night with me...'

Alex tautened, dark colour accentuating his hard cheekbones. 'You are even more drunk than I thought you were.'

Her glazed eyes fell from his. 'I've put my foot in my mouth—'

'I intend to put my fist in Marco's.'

'I was only joking.'

Alex pressed her towards the door. 'He wasn't...'

'H-honestly?' she stammered in disbelief.

'You think I'd be here if it wasn't true?'

He guided her out through the buzzing reception area. Her blitzed brain was endeavouring to absorb what he had confirmed. Alex Rossini *wanted* her. He found her desirable. What would have threatened and appalled her a mere twelve hours earlier now, for some reason, fascinated her. 'You were so kind this afternoon—'

'And I wouldn't be kind without a hidden agenda?'

'No,' she said without even thinking about it.

A chauffeur was standing by the door of a silver limousine. Sara climbed in, slid along the richly upholstered leather seat. Her luxurious surroundings made no impression on her at all. Don't think about Brian, don't think about Brian, she urged herself feverishly. 'Why didn't you...? I mean, you never showed—'

'Sara, I'm not a lovesick teenager. I find you physically very attractive. That is chemistry.'

'Sex.'

'Sex,' Alex agreed drily.

Was that the way Brian wanted Antonia? Did it matter whether it was love or infatuation or simply lust which had motivated him? Would love hurt any more than the way she was already feeling? Had it only been guilt which had made him chase out of the flat in her wake? *Stop it...stop it* a little voice shrieked inside her. It's over, Sara. Accept it. Alex was right. You could never trust Brian again.

'You think I'm very naïve,' Sara muttered, closing out the seething turmoil threatening her again.

'No. I don't think this is the time for this conversation.'

'I don't believe in love any more.' For hadn't Brian done all the right things? Romantic cards, constant phone calls. Last night he had been with *her*, holding hands, smiling...the consummate actor, and she had been the blind fool, for she had noticed nothing different.

'How would you like to sink into an alcoholic stupor and have a nice long sleep?' Alex enquired with unconcealed hope.

'Very, very much,' she whispered painfully.

The silence pulsed with undertones that she didn't understand.

'I really didn't know your feelings went this deep.' A grim laugh splintered from him.

She didn't show her feelings. She had learnt that young. But today she had been brutally wrenched out of her protective shell. 'How could you know?'

'I thought you were more in love with the bridal trappings...not to mention the wallpaper books, fabric swatches and paint-cards,' Alex enumerated with sardonic bite.

'I wanted a home that was really mine. Easy to mock what you've always had, Alex.' Sara shot him a look of angry intensity that challenged him and then tore her gaze away again, but he stayed etched in her mind's eye. The gleaming black hair, the slashing brows, the hard, arrogant slant of his mouth and nose. *Hard*—that was the definitive word. He might be possessed of a quite intoxicating masculine beauty but the raw stamp of power and fierce force of will overlaid those spectacular dark good looks like bonded steel.

Her head was pounding sickly. 'I'm not even asking you where we're going...'

'You're safe with me. Tonight you don't have to think for yourself.'

She closed her aching eyes. The one male in the world whom she would never, ever have trusted and yet all of a sudden she instinctively did trust him. Alex Rossini, protector. She ought to have laughed at the idea but instead she fell asleep.

Sara surfaced from a nightmare, shivering and perspiring. She sat up with a dizzy start and found herself in a completely unfamiliar room. The bedside lamps were

lit on either side of the wide divan bed. The sheet tangled
round her was silk. She lifted an uncertain hand to the
thin, strappy nightdress clinging to the damp thrust of
her breasts and fell still only when she saw the tall, dark
male rising from a chair in the shadows.

'Alex . . .' she whispered shakily as it all came back in
jagged bits and pieces and she breathed in sharply in
relief, helplessly reassured by his presence.

'Feel like something to eat?' He sounded so normal,
so casual.

'Where am I . . .? Oh, Lord, to have to *ask* that,' she
muttered between clenched teeth.

'This is my house. I didn't think leaving you alone in
the company apartment would be very wise—'

'Your dinner party.'

'Cancelled. Not one of my better ideas.'

From below the screen of her lashes she surveyed him
with inescapable fascination. Nothing seemed real—not
the day's events, certainly not the extraordinary alteration that had taken place in their relationship within
the space of hours. She had not looked before she'd leapt
today. He had looked for her, watched over her, kept
her safe. *Why*? Did he want her so much that he was
prepared to put up with her as she was now?

'I'll order some food.'

The door flipped quietly shut in his wake but still she
looked to where he had been. She had got blindly, foolishly drunk and Alex Rossini had picked up the pieces.
But he hadn't expected her to react that way. . . What
had he expected? Why should he have *expected* anything
when he couldn't have known what would happen to her
today? The dinner party—'Not one of my better ideas'.
He had talked almost as though the dinner party had
been stage-managed in advance for her entertainment,
which was crazy. She must have misunderstood him.

She slid out of bed. Her head was still swimming a
little. She grimaced at the foul taste in her mouth and
was exceedingly grateful to find a bathroom through the

other door that she had espied. Her own tousled reflection in the mirror shook her. Peeling off the nightdress, she switched on the shower and stepped into the
cubicle, grateful for the warm water and the rich lather
of the soap that would wash her clean.

Who had undressed her and put her to bed? Alex?
How strange that she shouldn't be plunged into stricken
mortification over the idea. Yesterday she would have
died a thousand deaths. Today—tonight—she knew that
she had already betrayed so much to Alex Rossini that
the once slavishly cherished sanctity of her own body no
longer seemed worthy of such earth-shattering
importance.

And why didn't she face it? She had very probably
driven Brian into Antonia's arms! She had refused to
sleep with him before they got married. Deaf to his every
protest, she had been determined to wait for their
wedding night, had smugly believed that the sexual restraint would lend an extra-special meaning to the vows
they would take. Only now there wasn't going to be a
wedding day... and it was cold comfort to acknowledge
that she had saved her virginity but lost the man she
loved. Maybe she had got exactly what she deserved.
She had put her wretched principles first and where had
it got her? She slid back into bed, forcing her cold face
into the pillow, raw with the bitter pain of rejection and
humiliation. Nothing was ever going to give her her pride
back.

She didn't hear the door open; she went rigid when
she was gathered up into strong male arms, and then
her nostrils flared on the scent of Alex and she trembled,
her arms uncoiling and curving round him very, very
slowly. No, I mustn't do this...she thought. But it felt
so good, so damned good to be held close. The breath
shortened in her dry throat. Her fingers splayed centimetre by centimetre across one powerful shoulder and
stayed there. She was almost paralysed by her
own daring.

The silence thundered in her ears.

He released his breath in a faint hiss and she could feel the savage tension in his taut, muscular frame and the pounding of his accelerated heartbeat against hers. And Sara smiled for the first time in hours with a sense of gratified wonder and curved even closer, her other hand sliding against his silk shirt-front, feeling the heat of his flesh burning through the fine fabric. His response was intoxicating.

'Is this a solo party...or a masquerade?' Alex demanded softly. 'I am not *him*. You will not close your eyes in my arms and pretend that I am.'

Shocked, she tipped her head back, eyes wide, and met a vibrant gold challenge. 'I know who you are,' she whispered dazedly, yet in his arms, even with her eyes open, she felt as if she was living some fantastic dream.

Lean hands closed gently round her wrists and pushed her back against the pillows. He curved one long-fingered hand to her cheekbone and held her still, raking her bewildered face with grim intensity. 'You want me to want you now,' he said tautly.

It was the truth, although she hadn't seen it for herself. Hectic colour lashed her cheeks beneath that appraisal. 'Yes...'

'Not like this,' Alex swore, his eloquent mouth hardening. 'And not tonight.'

She had been stumbling round like a clown half the day under his gaze. No doubt whatever imagined attraction he had endowed her with had evaporated fast when he had been faced with such pathetic reality. Alex Rossini was accustomed to sophisticated women and none of those experienced ladies would ever have made such a fool of herself in his presence as she had. As he released her a semi-hysterical laugh was torn from her. It came out of nowhere and shook her.

'Don't...' Alex reproved her thickly. 'I want to make love to you very badly. I've wanted you for a long time but I won't take advantage of you when you don't know what you're doing.'

But she *did* know, for she knew herself far better than he did and she wasn't the type to have an affair with her boss, or the sort of woman who longed to see herself made notorious in newsprint as Alex Rossini's latest bed-partner for a few adventurous weeks. There would be no tomorrow for them; there was only tonight. He couldn't take his eyes off her, she registered in fascination.

'Sara...?' he prompted rawly, his blunt cheekbones overlaid with dark colour and prominent with ferocious tension.

Green eyes gazed back at him in defiant challenge. 'One night... and it won't cost you two million. It won't cost you anything. I don't put a price on myself,' she told him with a bitter edge to her voice because she knew now that once she had put a price on her body and that price had been a wedding ring.

'*Cristo*...' Alex seethed down at her in sudden incredulous frustration. 'What's come over you that you're talking like this?'

Her jewel-like eyes were relentlessly nailed to his as an unfamiliar feeling of power took her over. 'I want...I want to be wanted tonight...'

'OK...' Alex sprang upright in one driven motion and stared fulminatingly down at her. 'But you remember that this is not how *I* wanted it to be between us.'

And how had he imagined it would be? The two million for one wild night? Had that been his sexual fantasy? Or a few candlelit dinners, a lot of Italian charm and compliments and so to bed? Alex usually conducted his affairs with style. With flowers, gifts, country weekends, cruises on his fabulous yacht, *Sea Spring*. This was more honest—much more honest—than either proposition and she did know exactly what she was doing, didn't she...? *Didn't* she? For an instant Sara had a frightening glimpse of her own emotional turmoil and knew that she was actually on the brink of an abyss, knew that she simply couldn't bear the thought of the long, lonely hours of the night which stretched ahead, knew that Alex's desire was balm to her savaged ego.

But had any woman but her ever wanted Alex Rossini for company rather than physical gratification? She wasn't expecting the latter, wasn't expecting any rolling waves to hit any metaphoric seashores, could be honest enough now to admit to herself that she had never been particularly interested in that aspect of human relations, even with Brian. It had been no sacrifice for *her* to practise celibacy. All that clumsy, awkward, heavy-breathing stuff had, frankly, left her cold, but she was intelligent enough to accept that other women didn't feel that way. She had often heard her own sex talk unashamedly about their sexual urges and once she had worried that there was something lacking in her because she did not feel the same needs as they apparently did. Then she had come to terms with her own essential coolness in that field.

She heard the shower switch off, the door open again, the sound of his footfalls on the thick carpet and thought, Dear heaven, what am I doing? Am I crazy, am I on the edge of a breakdown to be inviting an intimacy that I don't even want? And then Alex reached for her, pulling her up against him with a long, powerful arm. A stifled gasp of shock escaped her as he drew her into remorseless contact with every lean, hard line of his masculine physique. He rolled lithely over on the bed, taking her with him, and gazed down at her with burning golden eyes.

'You can change your mind,' he told her not quite evenly.

Eyes to drown in, eyes to tempt a saint, so wickedly beautiful in that hard male face that they took her breath away. Sara looked up at him, bereft of words, suddenly hopelessly entrapped by that all-enveloping gaze. She wondered, in a state of complete abstraction, what it would be like to be kissed by him, which was about as far as her craven imagination was inclined to take her.

'I want the lights on...I don't want you to forget...*bella mia*,' he murmured with a sudden fractured roughness that tingled down her spinal cord and made her shiver. Forget what? she almost asked, but she couldn't make her voice work and it didn't seem important.

He wound his forefinger into a silky strand of her hair and slowly lowered his dark head, almost as if he expected her to shout, No! at the last possible moment, but Sara was wholly entranced. *Bella*...beautiful, she was savouring dreamily.

And then she found out what his mouth felt like on hers and she froze when his tongue probed between her parted lips. She had never liked *that*...but his sensual mouth became more insistent, more demanding and she trembled, pulses suddenly racing, heart accelerating madly, and she discovered that she had no resistance, no urge to pull back from that intoxicating pleasure.

Her head swam, a kind of stunned disbelief threatening to demand utterance, but he kissed her breathless and it would have taken restraint to initiate dialogue and she had none at all. She was carried blindly from one seductive kiss to the next, as badly hooked as an addict on heady delight.

Sure fingers moved against the full thrust of her breasts and a surge of such tormenting excitement took her in its grasp that her mind was a complete blank. She couldn't think, indeed she could barely breathe as she felt her own flesh swell, her nipples pinching into tight, prominent buds. He ran his mouth down the extended line of her throat, strung a line of inflaming kisses along her collar-bone, dallied on pulse-points and places she didn't know she had until that moment, and left her weak but with every skin cell alive with quivering, devastating anticipation.

'Look at me...' Alex demanded.

Her lashes flew up on command. She looked, lingered, drowned in smouldering gold. 'Alex,' she mumbled shakily, the fingers of one seeking hand pushing through his thick dark hair, shaping his head in an involuntary caress that also held him fast.

A brilliant smile flashed across his sensual mouth. He ran the tip of his tongue teasingly down the valley between her breasts and she shivered violently. 'Alex,' she said again without the smallest shade of doubt.

He peeled the nightdress out of his determined path, slowly shaped the quivering thrust of her achingly sensitive flesh with expert hands and then imprisoned a throbbing pink nipple in his mouth, suckling hungrily at the tender bud. Her whole body jerked in the surge of scorching heat that he evoked, the sudden, shattering, first-time pull of nerve-endings awakening to sexual passion taking her over. What remained of her control vanished simultaneously.

She heard a voice moaning, didn't recognise it as her own, her fingers tightly gripping the hot, sleek smoothness of his shoulders as her back arched. Pleasure she had never dreamt of was shooting through her in agonising waves and there was hardly a pause between one peak and the next. She twisted beneath him, couldn't stay still, wanting, needing, her thighs trembling, tightening on the ache building inside her.

He said something caressing in Italian, and the last thought that she would afterwards recall was that Italian was definitely the language of love in that incredibly rich, deep voice of his, and then he skimmed a hand through the damp curls at the base of her taut stomach and the world became a delirious, multicoloured shower of lights behind her lowered eyelids as he discovered the moist heat at the very heart of her. She cried out, gasped, shuddered. The hungry ache fired higher and higher, the strength of her own need biting so deep that it hurt, driving her to the edge of torment and making her plant desperate little kisses over any part of him that she could reach, her tongue tasting him, her teeth grazing him as her slender hips rose pleadingly against his most intimate caresses.

'Wait...' Alex groaned raggedly.

A split second after he drew back from her Sara tugged him back again with insistent hands and covered his mouth wildly, feverishly with her own, automatically utilising everything that he had taught her to keep him in the circle of her arms. He stiffened and then with an earthy groan surrendered with raw enthusiasm, his long, muscular length shuddering as his hands settled on her thighs and he moved against her, freeing her swollen lips, gazing down at her with ferocious hunger. 'If this is a dream, I don't ever want to wake up,' he confessed with passionate conviction.

'Alex...' she gasped tautly, her entire quivering body reaching up to his in helpless need, reacting with liquid-honey-enticement to the tantalising, hot, hard probe of his flesh against hers.

The surge of pain caught her on the crest of tortured anticipation. She gasped in shock, eyes flying wide to meet similar shock in his startled gaze. *'Cristo cara...'* he said in hoarse disbelief, but the momentary frown etched between his ebony brows was swiftly wiped away and the dark eyes glittered more golden than ever.

And then he moved again lithely, powerfully deepening his penetration, and a truly stunning wave of breathtaking sensation swept her back into that wild oblivion where only the demands of her own hungry body held sway. With every driving thrust he took her with him, made the fire burning inside her flame ever higher, ever more unbearably, until her teeth clenched and her heartbeat thundered and her nails raked fiercely down his damp back because the wild, hot pleasure that went on and on only made her more desperate. The explosive burst of her own climax was electrifying. It blew her apart, left her trembling in devastated aftershock from a sheer overload of pleasure.

'I feel better in my bed.' Alex was sweeping her up, letting his mouth caress hers again tenderly, then there was movement. That was all her punch-drunk senses could recognise. She felt the faint chill of colder air and then a cool sheet against her back before the heat and muscularity of Alex connected with her again.

'Don't go to sleep,' he instructed her, his dark drawl impossibly vibrant and wide awake as he wrapped his arms around her possessively and vented a deeply satisfied sigh of slumberous relaxation.

Not waves on shores so much as a golden sun of glory around which she had revolved, she conceded sleepily. So much effort to think . . . so much easier simply to feel, and she felt wonderfully at peace.

'We spend the weekend on the yacht. I'm in Paris on Monday . . . you'll *love* Paris, *cara*. What do you think?' he probed.

What did she think? Sara struggled valiantly to think. She thought that he sounded as if he had closed a tremendously difficult and lucrative business deal which had lost some poor fool a fortune and made him another mountain of money that he didn't need: immensely, shamelessly self-satisfied. At that point her brain switched off and she shifted with positive contentment into the warm, comforting solidarity of him.

Her nose twitched on the heady scent of flowers. She lifted heavy eyelids slowly, focused on a giant, beribboned basket of flowers and then another basket . . . and then another. Her mouth went dry. She woke up in a hurry, jerking upright in an unfamiliar bed in an unfamiliar bedroom and gaped at all the flowers surrounding her. Her attention lodged on a man's silk tie lying in a tiny splash of crimson on top of a dense, creamy carpet and her heart plunged as if she had gone down at supersonic speed in a lift.

She nearly fell out of the bed in her haste to vacate it. Memory took her back and then forward. She turned as white as a sheet and suddenly knew without any prompting what being sober *really* felt like. A case she recognised as her own was sitting by the window. With a pained groan of disbelief, she stared at it. He had somehow got her clothes out of the flat? Oh, dear Lord, what had she done? What *had* she done?

With frantic hands she tore into the case. Taped to the inner lid was a big piece of paper, slashed with Antonia's untidy scrawl. 'What the hell is going on?' it said.

Sara grabbed up a handful of clothes and dived into the *en suite* bathroom. She studied herself in the mirror—red, swollen mouth, shadowed eyes, wildly tousled black hair. Trollop, tart, she castigated herself with tears of rage and shame burning her eyes. How could she have behaved like that with Alex Rossini? She wanted to sink into a great black hole—no, she wanted to put him into a great black hole and pour tons of concrete over him so that he could never escape and she would never have to meet his eyes again!

Thankfully he had already left for the office... Oh, dear heaven, *the office*! It was already after nine. She would say that she had missed the bus. Nobody would think anything of that; nobody need ever know... but if she had had any choice she wouldn't have walked into Rossini Industries ever again. However, there would certainly be talk if she suddenly disappeared and failed to work out the last ten days of her notice—much better to grit her teeth and finish her time there. In any case, she conceded bitterly, she badly needed her month's salary because her bank account was almost empty.

Fumbling, with little of her usual dexterity, she contrived to confine her hair into a murderously tight bun at the nape of her neck.

She crept out of the bedroom, her arm nearly falling off from the weight of the case she was hauling with her. Tight-mouthed, she dragged it along to the landing at the top of the stairs. With every movement, she was more and more aware of the complaint of newly discovered muscles in unmentionable places and the undeniable ache in the least mentionable place of all, and her rage thundered higher with very step.

'*Buon giorno, cara...*'

Her throat thickened. Slowly she straightened, stricken eyes flying to the tall, devastatingly attractive male standing at the head of the staircase.

'I was coming up to see if you wanted to join me for breakfast...but we can do without the luggage,' Alex assured her very softly, measuring dark eyes speeding over her furiously flushed face and lingering with incipient shrewdness. 'Don't do it—don't say what's brimming on your lips... Don't disappoint me, *cara.*'

She wanted to kick him down the stairs. A temper that she had never had any trouble controlling until now was suddenly threatening to explode. She sucked in air, freezing her facial muscles. 'I happen to be late for work, Mr Rossini.' Ice dripped from every syllable.

She hit her lowest ebb as she watched his sensual mouth twist and then compress. She didn't need to be told how ridiculous she had sounded. Then his strong dark face tautened. Brilliant dark eyes rested on her. 'Sara...I want you to count to ten and think about last night without prejudice. Is that possible for you?'

'No,' she said woodenly, honestly, dragging her mortified gaze from his—an act which took so much willpower that she felt drained.

'We shared something very special which I don't want...or intend...to lose. It doesn't matter that you were on the rebound...the only thing that matters is how we both feel now,' Alex drawled very quietly. 'Clean page, open book.'

'Close it,' Sara said between gritted teeth.

'I don't mind you cutting off your nose to spite your face...*per Dio*, I mind very much if you attempt to make a similar sacrifice of me!' Alex covered the space between them in one long, fluid stride.

'I made a mistake, damn you!' Sara spat, tears scorching her eyes.

'No, *cara*. That's where you're wrong. What happened between us was no mistake—not for me and not for you either.'

'Am I entitled to voice an opinion of my own?'

'Not right now...no.' Alex lifted the case from her, set it arrogantly aside. 'The prudish streak is threatening to go on the rampage.'

Sara flinched as though he had struck her.

'*Bella mia...*' Alex sighed reprovingly, smoothing long brown fingers caressingly over one pale, taut cheekbone, his accented drawl low and very soft. Even though she didn't want to stand there and allow him to touch her again, something frightening, something stronger than she was kept her still, unresisting, her slender length leaning involuntarily closer as if she wanted to curve into that hand and stretch like a sensual cat. 'Don't leave. I promise not to try and force anything more. You need time and space to think. I'll give it to you. I'll be patient...I'll stay in the background.'

'Alex...' Her voice fractured as she fought to free herself from the spell he cast even while she mentally reeled at the impossible image of Alex Rossini endeavouring to sink into the woodwork.

'There's nothing to be ashamed of, nothing to regret—'

'But I don't *want* this!' Sara gasped, suddenly finding that freedom to speak her own thoughts. She jerked her head away from him. 'I don't want to have an affair with you. Last night was madness—'

'Sweet insanity that worked like a dream... Don't deny what you're feeling right now.'

'I feel nothing...*nothing*!' she swore violently, and, snatching up her case again with an energy born of desperation, she started down the stairs.

'Sara, you cannot possibly go back into the office after this.'

He caught up with her in the hall. A firm hand closed round hers and tugged her back and round to face him again.

'You think I'm going to be your mistress, you think wrong!' Sara threw at him rawly.

'What did I tell you to be sure to remember today? That this was not how I wanted it to be between us,' Alex reminded her with controlled anger. 'But you wouldn't settle for anything less and now you blame me for it. That's very female but bloody unfair.'

Her shocked eyes fell from his. 'I'm not blaming you. I just want to forget this happened, that's all.'

'But I will not play that game... and take your hair out of that excruciatingly ugly old-maid style!' Alex suddenly gritted, and hauled her even closer, banding one strong arm round her narrow back as his free hand roved free to the thick coil of hair and released it from its confinement. 'You're a beautiful young woman; rejoice in that beauty... don't stifle it!'

'Let go of me!' Sara told him shrilly.

'All I want to do is take you back to bed,' Alex confided in an undertone of angrily suppressed passion as he brought her up against him, a lean hand splaying to the feminine swell of her hips with a lover's intimacy.

Appalled cat-green eyes collided with his gaze and the atmosphere sizzled. She blinked bemusedly, feeling the piercingly sweet heat reawaken low in the pit of her stomach, the sudden ache of her nipples as her breasts stirred beneath her bra. Her soft mouth trembled. Alex smiled lazily down at her, shifted with fluid emphasis against her and she felt the force of his arousal with shock. Her lower limbs turned to cotton wool. Her ability to breathe and think for herself diminished with terrifying rapidity. 'Stop it...' she whispered breathlessly.

'One kiss, *bella mia*, and I'll let you go into work,' he bargained mockingly.

'No!' she spat as her heartbeat pounded like a trapped bird in a cage.

'Stubborn...' Alex breathed thickly, amused. 'You want that kiss as much as I do.'

'I'm sorry...I didn't realise...I used the rear entrance,' another voice intervened.

Alex's hand dropped instantly. Sara sprang back from him, eyes wide with horror when she saw Pete Hunniford standing several feet away, his mobile features momentarily transfixed with incredulity and then swiftly rearranged into total impassivity.

CHAPTER THREE

SARA stood there like a graven image as Pete handed a file to Alex.

'Sara needs a lift back to the office.' Alex quirked a sardonic black brow as he glanced reflectively at her. 'Unless you've changed your mind, *cara*?'

'No.' She wrenched open the heavy front door for herself, and frankly couldn't get out of the huge house quickly enough.

Alex dropped an arm round her and walked her out onto the top step, seemingly indifferent to a degree of icy, repulsing rigidity which would have frozen off the continuing advances of any normal male. 'Lunch at one... Sara?'

Sara was staring in consternation at the man who had darted out from his position by the railings and focused a camera on them both. *Click*! Grinning, he then ran across the street and jumped into a car. 'How unfortunate,' Alex said, and he didn't even attempt to sound convincing.

The thick atmosphere between Sara and Pete on the drive back to the office would have defied the sharpest knife.

'Right,' Pete began grimly. 'Now the first thing you do is lie like a trooper to dear Brian. You worked late, had to stay over... you say I was there too. You do not confess; do you understand that, Sara? Believe me, Brian does not want the whole truth and nothing but the truth in this instance. That story covers you on all fronts. The paparazzi are always watching Alex. So there'll be a photo of you emerging from his house at ten in the morning in tomorrow's papers... What does that prove? Nothing.'

42

Paper-pale, Sara parted her lips, unsurprised by his cynical advice but deeply embarrassed by his frankness. 'Pete, I—'

'I can't believe it... *You!*' he muttered, shaking his smoothly styled head. 'I thought you were bombproof around Alex. I feel responsible. I only gave you the job because you were engaged. Only the day before yesterday you were handing Alex a cup of coffee as though he was the carrier of some dread social disease, and this morning...?'

'Please, let's not talk about it,' Sara mumbled. She thought of yesterday's sunny awakening, her blinkered innocence of what the day would bring. And then this morning's devastating dawn.

'Obviously Alex finally made a move on you. Well, heaven knows, I've been waiting for it to happen. I've worked around Alex a long time. Believe it or not, I *like* Alex... but if he looked at my sister the way he's always looked at you I'd lock her up and throw away the key... because Alex is very bad news with women. He's emotionally cold and detached. I've seen him in action too many times not to know that—'

'Pete...' Had everyone *but* her been aware of Alex's interest in her?

'Your two predecessors fell head over heels for him and made a blasted nuisance of themselves! I thought you had more sense.'

Sense? When and where had sense figured in yesterday's turmoil? She felt cheap and stupid and desperately ashamed of herself. Was that prudish? But she couldn't discard the values of a lifetime overnight. She had invited...no, far worse, virtually *pleaded* for Alex's sexual attentions. She had thrown herself at his head. Her stomach cramped with nausea.

How could she have done that? Why had she done it? Had she sunk so low in self-esteem that she had been grateful to Alex Rossini for finding her desirable? Had she needed the proof that she could still attract a man after seeing Brian in Antonia's arms? Or on some level had she sought revenge for that agonising betrayal? If that had been her motivation, she was now discovering that revenge was a two-edged sword that could turn back on you and inflict piercing pain and regret.

When she and Pete arrived at the office Gina, the svelte receptionist, gave her a curious, veiled look as she murmured a greeting. Two executive secretaries were out in the corridor having a close conversation, but fell silent as she walked past. Their greetings were very muted indeed. Sara didn't have to wait long to find out why.

'Miss Lacey?' A uniformed waiter whipped the covers from a selection of food on a heated trolley. 'Breakfast, compliments of Mr Rossini.'

'Bloody hell,' Pete said only half under his breath as he drew to a halt beside her. Clearing his throat, he said rather loudly, 'I hope there's enough for two. Working so late, I slept in—didn't have time for much this morning.'

Sara was so taken aback that she couldn't even throw Pete a look of gratitude for his efforts to cover up for her. In any case, who was likely to believe that Alex had demanded Pete to leave his wife's side and work overtime last night?

She sank down behind her desk, watched numbly as the food was served. She hadn't eaten since breakfast yesterday, but she might have eaten last night had she not been far more intent on seducing Alex Rossini into spending the night with her. Hectic colour fired her creamy skin. Alex hadn't wanted her to return to the office. He would be well aware that such an extravagant gesture would create gossip—the kind of gossip that Sara shrank from. Could he be cruel enough to use that as a weapon against her?

'What did Molly have... a boy or a girl?' she asked, striving valiantly for normality.

'Didn't Alex tell you? He was on the phone a good ten minutes with me yesterday...' Pete flushed. 'Sorry— little girl. We're going to call her Flora.'

'Congratulations.' Sara lifted her knife and fork, her fingers all thumbs.

'Sara...you look like death warmed over,' Pete said, tight-mouthed.

'I'm fine.'

She wondered if she would ever feel fine again. As she forced herself to eat, she drowned in a torrent of brutally unwelcome erotic images. She sat there growing ever more appalled, ever more bewildered by the wanton creature that she had become in Alex Rossini's arms. If only it had been unpleasant, sordid, disappointing even... She hated him all the more for the fact that it hadn't been! She did not think that she could ever forgive herself for finding Alex Rossini more physically exciting than the man she loved. What did that say about her?

Maybe her aunt had been right about her all along. Janice Dalton had regularly lectured Sara on the dangers of promiscuity. As a quiet, far from precocious teenager, Sara had found those sessions deeply humiliating and she had bitterly resented the knowledge that the older woman feared the hereditary factor. 'I don't want you turning out like your mother did,' her aunt had told her. Had the mother she barely remembered slept around? The concept had been distastefully implied more than once. There had always been a grim irony in Janice Dalton's blind refusal to see how her own daughter lived her life.

'Sara?' Pete was in the doorway.

Sara glanced up from the accounts that she was checking. Her job covered a lot of ground. She had overall responsibility for the day-to-day running of Alex's various homes round the world. She dealt with minor household crises, changes of staff, repair and main- tenance bills, indeed all the boring minutiae that Alex didn't have time to deal with but which had to be dealt with if the smooth running of his domestic arrangements was to continue with the faultless efficiency that he took for granted.

'I understand that Alex gave an order that you were to receive no personal calls yesterday afternoon.'

'Did he?'

Pete grimaced. 'Brian is on his way up in the lift.'

Every scrap of colour ebbed from her cheeks.

'See him in here. I'll take myself off.'

'But Alex—'

'So Alex doesn't allow personal visitors...but then Alex isn't in yet.'

Sara stood up slowly. Brian appeared on the threshold. He looked as if he'd been up all night—pasty pale, tense, his eyes bloodshot. Pete closed the door on his way out, giving her a ludicrous thumbs-up sign behind Brian's back.

'Sara...' Brian swallowed. 'What do I say to you?'

It was as if a glass wall stood between them, as though a thousand years had passed since yesterday. 'There's nothing to say.' She felt nothing, absolutely nothing at all, only a terrible emptiness.

'She'd been chasing after me for weeks,' he muttered unevenly. 'I'm not making excuses...but—'

'It gave you a kick because she wasn't interested three years ago.'

He flushed and then nodded with compressed lips.

'And you just couldn't help yourself.'

His strained brown eyes met hers. 'That's where you're wrong. I don't even like Toni. I know what she's like. It was just...you know...a physical thing. Damn it, Sara, how do I say to you that I just wanted to go to bed with her and then forget she existed? But that's how it was!' he told her with sudden fierceness, and she could feel him willing her to believe him. 'There was no emotion involved. I know you have to think that's disgusting but it's *you* that I love, *you* that I want to marry.'

His pleading gaze met hers. A knife twisted inside her then. 'You have to know that that is impossible now,' she managed shakily.

'Look, let me tell you it all from the beginning—'

'No, I don't want to know! It's upsetting for both of us to drag this out. I couldn't ever *forget* ... you see,' she said chokily, and then she remembered Alex and what she herself had done and spun away, too upset to say anything more.

The door clicked open. Alex lounged there, his densely lashed dark eyes, no shade of gold in their depths, shooting to her with a burning anger that didn't show on his strong dark face but which Sara discovered that she could *feel* with every fibre of her shrinking body. The atmosphere vibrated and she registered in stricken bewilderment that that one scorching look from Alex had filled *her* with guilt. Alex was outraged to find her even talking to Brian.

'I believe you've overstayed your welcome, Shorter,' Alex drawled chillingly. 'Don't come here again.'

Complete bewilderment flashed across Brian's face.

'Alex ...' Sara whispered in shock, for in that threatening gaze she recognised the kind of savage, territorial instincts which more properly belonged in the jungle, not in civilised society. She had the frightening suspicion that if Brian said one word out of line Alex would use it as an excuse to throw him down the lift shaft.

'What's going on here?' Brian asked, shaking his blond head. 'I don't understand...'

Alex strolled forward like a prowling panther and slid a fluid arm round Sara's rigid back. 'Sara and I are going for lunch. You're wasting your time,' he delivered very drily.

Brian's jaw dropped. 'Sara?'

Sara didn't know where to put herself. Alex took care of that problem too. He simply swept her out of the office, down the corridor and into the lift. Before the doors slid shut she had a perfect view of Gina's incredulous expression.

'Did you return the ring?' Alex enquired flatly.

Sara finally unglued her tongue from the roof of her shocked mouth. 'How dare you do that to me? How *dare* you speak to Brian like that?'

'How long was he in there with you?' Alex demanded. 'Evidently long enough to tell you a sob story!'

'It's none of your business how long I was with him.'

'You slept in my arms all last night. If that doesn't make it my business, what does?' he responded with devastating frankness. '*Dio* . . . I'm sure you didn't tell him that.'

A tide of painful heat engulfed every inch of Sara's exposed body. Alex Rossini had been put on earth purely to torment her, she thought in anguished disbelief. He steamrollered over every sensibility she possessed.

'I presume you *did* tell him that he was yesterday's news?'

His expectant silence sizzled.

'What does it matter to you whether I did or not?' she flung at him wildly.

'I don't share my women. It's an old Italian custom,' Alex returned with sardonic bite.

Sara stumbled out into the cool of the underground car park. 'I am not one of your women!'

He swung round. 'Then what are you?'

Her eyes clashing with that coolly enquiring dark gaze, Sara went rigid, her breath catching in her throat. 'I'm in love with another man—'

'Who's already history.' Alex studied her with cool intent. 'A man you never even shared a bed with. What kind of love was that?'

'The kind of love I'm sure you couldn't understand!'

'Pure, perfect love,' Alex mocked. 'It had to be perfect for you, Sara...that was the most important part, wasn't it?'

'I don't know what you're talking about.'

He pressed her into the waiting limousine. 'The white wedding, the virgin sacrifice. It's medieval. What were you going to do if you finally got into the marriage bed and found you didn't like what he did there?'

'Don't be disgusting!' Sara gasped.

'You'd have been a martyr. You'd have gritted your teeth and mentally flipped through a wallpaper book while the poor devil got on with it.'

Outrage leapt through her. 'I refuse to listen to this.'

'You were shocked by your own response last night...'

'No!' she gasped, jerking her dark head away, trembling with the force of her own jagged reactions. Emotions were all churning about on the surface—emotions she wasn't used to handling.

'And you weren't the only one shocked,' Alex breathed, his dark drawl fracturing. 'It never occurred to me that you could still be a virgin, and I would never have got into that bed with you had I known that. I'm not in the habit of taking advantage of untutored innocence.'

'I don't want to talk about it.' Her strained voice quivered. 'I don't even know what I'm doing here with you.'

'You wanted an escape from Brian,' Alex told her grimly. 'That's why you're here.'

Dazedly she closed her eyes. He might as well have reached inside her and read a label. Was she so transparent? Until he'd said it she hadn't even appreciated why she had allowed Alex's arrogant intervention. It had been easier, less painful than prolonging an encounter which could only have gone round in ever more distressing circles. Had Antonia been Brian's dream woman? A dream he had finally set aside? Had he knowingly settled for second best when he'd chosen Sara—someone who shared his interests, his outlook, his goals, but still a woman as different from Antonia as any woman could be? There had been nothing left to talk about with Brian.

'You don't even blame him, do you?' Alex murmured.

Sara searched herself, learnt that once again Alex could hit the target with disturbing accuracy. Her anger had settled into sad acceptance. 'She's very beautiful, very tempting,' she said gruffly.

'She's a blue-eyed blonde with good teeth and long legs. There's a lot of them out there,' Alex returned dismissively.

Momentarily she was transfixed by such a description of her glamorous cousin. Then she reminded herself that on Alex's international scale of beautiful women Antonia might well strike him as being not that special... only that did not explain—indeed it made all the more impossible to understand—*why* Alex should think a five-foot-one-inch brunette secretary worthy of such attention as she was receiving!

And then she understood why and was astonished that she had not solved the riddle sooner. Alex got bored so easily with women. Listening to Pete, wryly concealing her awareness of his helpless masculine envy, she had heard time and time again about just how eager women were to attract Alex Rossini's attention. Sara's greatest attraction could only have been her lack of interest.

Her apparent indifference had singled her out from the rest of the female staff. She couldn't think of a single one who didn't go a little fluttery in Alex's presence. Even happily married, older women were *aware* of Alex's undeniable sexual charge... but Sara had blocked her awareness out, scornfully denying her own instinctively physical response to those spectacular dark good looks of his. Stubborn self-discipline had made it possible for her to close him out...until yesterday, when alcohol and shock had decimated her natural defences.

Alex assisted her out of the car, the warmth of his hand on her arm making her shiver and stiffen. She wanted nothing more to do with him. She had to tell him that. Very possibly he felt grimly responsible for her after what had happened between them. After all, she had turned out to be far less sexually experienced than he had cynically assumed.

The stylish restaurant was disconcertingly empty. Sara blinked as she sank into the chair pulled out for her. A pianist was playing quietly in the corner. Waiters *en masse* engulfed them in the most expensive variety of silent service.

'Where is everyone?' she asked weakly.

'I wanted privacy for us to talk . . . and I didn't think you would wish to return to my house.'

He had paid for the privilege of an empty room for her benefit? She swallowed hard. A light first course was swiftly served. Alex lounged back with a glass of wine in one shapely hand and surveyed her with immense calm. 'Eat,' he encouraged her softly.

'Let's get the talking over with,' she suggested brittlely.

A rueful smile curved his wide, sensual mouth. 'Sometimes you are very young, *cara*.'

'Just not used to this kind of treatment.'

'Very, very young,' Alex said wryly. 'And if you looked in the mirror without superimposing your cousin's standard of attractiveness you would see what I see. Perfect bone structure, eyes with the colour and depth of emeralds, translucent skin, a wonderfully sultry mouth and a figure that would tempt a saint from celibacy . . . and I am no saint, *bella mia*.'

Her mouth went dry, soft pink highlighting her cheekbones.

'When I look at you, I see a very lovely woman who walks, talks and behaves as if she's very plain and ordinary. That was what first drew my attention—that complete lack of self-awareness. You made me curious. I thought at first that it was an act, designed to actually attract attention . . .' As she stiffened he shifted a lithe hand, silencing her. 'Then I watched you look back at me and freeze and I knew that whatever you were you weren't indifferent.'

'If you're trying to say that I actually asked for—'

'If your wedding plans hadn't fallen through I would never have approached you,' Alex asserted softly. 'But no man who desires a woman ignores an opportunity when it comes his way. I didn't plan to take you to bed last night...it was too soon and, in the light of your inexperience, most ill judged, but I had no idea that I would be the first. Don't try to turn what we shared into a tawdry one-night stand. It wasn't, and what is more you know it wasn't.'

Sara dropped her head, forced against her volition to recall his lovemaking, a helpless curl of heat igniting in the pit of her stomach, making her pale and tauten in angry rejection of her body's weakness. 'But that doesn't change how I feel and think. We have different standards. What happened,' she framed tightly, 'shouldn't have happened.'

'But it did and there's no going back.'

'Maybe there wouldn't be if I fancied myself in love with you or something like that.' Her skin warmed, her generous mouth tightening. 'But I don't!'

'Love!' Alex repeated with audible exasperation.

'Obviously not something that comes into your affairs and probably never has done!' She had forced herself to be as honest as she could be. A sexual relationship without any deeper feelings was not for her. She might have leapt out of the frying-pan into the fire last night but she had enough strength of will to admit her own error and still stand her ground.

Alex vented a curiously chilling laugh, his dark eyes as hard as gemstones as he gazed back at her. 'Oh, I've been in love, Sara...a lot more deeply in love than I suspect you have ever been. I was nineteen. She was ten years older. It lasted two fantastic years and then one morning I woke up and she wasn't there any more. I spent six months trying to find her and at the end of that six months I would still have given every penny I possessed to have her back... Now that *is* love.'

Sara was shaken by the confession. For a split second she found herself envisaging Alex as the adoring, very vulnerable satellite of an older woman, but her imagination could not hold that image for long. At thirty-four there was nothing of the boy left in Alex. He was an overwhelmingly self-assured adult male. 'Why did she leave?' she heard herself ask, unable to stifle a flare of natural curiosity.

'She convinced herself that she was wrong for me.' Alex shrugged a broad shoulder, his mobile mouth twisting. 'But she also helped me to free myself from any illusions about love. Take a degree of mutual respect and liking and add in sexual attraction and you have a far more secure basis than you'll ever find with love.'

'I don't believe that.'

'Yet you had your illusions smashed only yesterday,' Alex reminded her with velvet-smooth cruelty. 'You took him for granted. You instinctively trusted him not to betray you. You built a whole rack of unreal expectations on the basis of the belief that love conquers all. Now, if you hadn't been *in* love, you wouldn't have made such sweeping assumptions and you wouldn't have felt so safe that you were blind to the signs that his attention was straying.'

'There may be a certain amount of truth in that but I would still say that for most people the benefits of loving and being loved more than outweigh the risks.'

'The feel-good factor,' Alex slotted in with satire. 'But whether you like it or not we both felt very good last night . . . and love had nothing whatsoever to do with it.'

Sara reddened furiously, loathing and helplessly resenting the way he kept on backing her into corners and arguing with her. Brian and she had almost never argued. She had seen that as a symbol of the strength of their relationship, a sign that they were wonderfully well matched. No doubt another one of the illusions of love which Alex had so coolly delineated.

'Emotionally cold and detached,' Pete had said. For the first time she really saw that aspect of Alex, and it sent a cold tingle down her spine as she contrasted that cool intellect with the apparent warmth and undeniable physical passion that he had shown her yesterday. No, she wouldn't like to be the fool who fell in love with Alex Rossini. The warmth could only have been an illusion, aimed to impress and reassure.

'Last night was last night—time out of time if you want to call it that,' Sara breathed. 'But I won't have an affair with you and I won't be your mistress either.'

'Why not?' Alex said lazily.

Her control snapped. 'Because we have nothing in common. Because we live in different worlds with different values—'

'But *not* because you're not interested.'

Silently fuming, Sara settled back into the limousine. 'Will you allow me to work out my notice without harassment of any kind?'

'Breakfast...was harassment?'

She bit her lower lip and tasted blood. 'You know what I mean...'

'Is what people might think so important to you that you would allow it to rule your life?'

'That's not fair!'

Alex reached for her clenched fingers where they rested on the seat. Momentarily she attempted to draw back from the contact and then, for a reason she could not begin to comprehend, her fingers stayed where they were, curled within his larger hand. She trembled; she didn't know what was happening to her. She had a sudden, terrifying urge to throw herself on Alex and sob her heart out. In all her life she had never felt more confused. He drew her relentlessly closer.

'Alex...no...' she whispered pleadingly.

But Alex didn't listen. He twined lean fingers into her fall of hair, tugging her round to face him. Her eyes burned as she met his shimmering gold enquiry and every tiny muscle tensed. Her pulsebeat thumped at the foot of her throat, a terrible excitement rising inside her no matter how hard she fought to suppress it. 'No...' she said again, as much for her own benefit as for his.

But an aching, compulsive wanting held her still. In dazed silence she recognised the shocking strength of promptings entirely new to her experience. Alex lowered his dark head and took her mouth with hungry urgency. Fire in the hold, she thought wildly, madly, feeling the instantaneous charge of her own helpless response. She wanted to grip him, hold him, mesh with every hard, muscular angle of his lean, virile length. The scent of him, the touch of him inflamed her senses with a drowning passion that was utterly self-absorbed. Tiny little sounds escaped her throat. Hot, electrifying pleasure engulfed her with every thrust of his tongue.

Her fingers slid with shameless hunger beneath his silk shirt, skimming luxuriantly over skin as smooth as velvet, feeling the taut contraction of his sleek muscles as he jerked and groaned beneath her exploration. He swept her up and pulled her down on top of him, expert hands gliding up the quivering stretch of her thighs, hitching up her confining skirt and then bringing her down again, sealing her into raw contact with the hard, throbbing length straining against his zip.

Shuddering, Alex released her swollen mouth, eyes of smouldering gold blazing over her rapt face. 'Come home with me...lie in bed with me...forget everything else,' he breathed raggedly.

In that split second the passenger door beside him sprung open with a thick clunk. Sara focused dazedly on his chauffeur's mirror-shiny shoes standing on the pavement and then she leapt off Alex with an agility and speed that a mountain goat would have envied, almost falling out of the limousine in her desperate haste to vacate it. Alex grated out something, called her name, but Sara kept on walking, right on past the clutch of

Rossini employees who were still staring open-mouthed and incredulous at what they had witnessed.

'Pete...' she said ten minutes later when she had tracked him down, 'I'm afraid I'm about to leave you in the lurch. I think it's time I went home.'

CHAPTER FOUR

'HEAVEN knows, Brian's entitled to an explanation. You've behaved disgracefully!' Janice Dalton railed in angry condemnation. 'The whole village is talking...and how do you think the Shorters feel about all this? They treated you like a daughter!'

'I'm sorry,' Sara whispered shakily.

'You *lied* to me. You told me that you and Brian had decided that you couldn't get married; you didn't have the decency to tell me or him that there was another man involved!'

Say nothing, don't argue and the sooner it will blow over. But after three solid days of recriminations following the publication of that wretched photo of her with Alex that belief was beginning to wear more than a little thin. It had not occurred to Sara when she'd decided to leave London and come home that she might find herself cast as the guilty partner. Brian was playing the martyr, the innocent...letting her take all the flak.

'Give it a rest, Ma.' Antonia appeared in the kitchen doorway, wearing her sunniest and most generous smile. 'At least the wedding invitations weren't in the post.'

'I'll bring the washing in.' Sara headed for the back door with alacrity. When she hit the fresh air, she drank in deeply.

'Blood will out, it seems ...' Her aunt's strained voice carried out through the window. 'But nobody could have been more careful than I was raising Sara...'

Sara moved out of earshot and began to take the washing off the line. It was a beautiful May day and she couldn't even appreciate it. She felt like a rat in a trap. The nightmare just seemed to go on and on. Antonia had driven down from London only an hour ago, perfectly groomed, blonde mane fresh from the hairdresser's, not a frazzled nerve in sight. Her cousin simply took it for granted that Sara would not dare to reveal the fact that she had found her in bed with Brian.

But then two wrongs did not make a right. Brian and Antonia's betrayal did not justify her own behaviour with Alex Rossini. But she wasn't trying to excuse herself any more. One misjudged night would not bring her world to an end. What tormented her was the bitter knowledge that Alex's intrusion on the scene had turned what would have been a simple broken engagement into a positive disaster. Her aunt and uncle were outraged by the belief that she had deceived Brian and then dumped him in apparent pursuit of a rich tycoon. That the aforementioned rich tycoon had then seemingly abandoned her was her aunt's sole consolation. Janice Dalton liked to see bad behaviour rewarded by just desserts.

Alex... She tensed, a ground swell of uneasy confusion engulfing her. Sometimes running away was the only way to protect yourself. She did not regret walking out of Rossini Industries that same day. It had been the only possible solution. She had made an absolute ass of herself and that had hit her pride hard, but nobody had ever died from reaping a salutary lesson in common sense.

She couldn't handle Alex Rossini. She couldn't handle a passion that smashed every safe boundary that she had ever observed. Alex had viewed her as an entertaining challenge. Alex had made her a target, amused by the unfamiliar cut and thrust of actually having to try and talk a woman into continuing to share his bed. But ultimately Alex had simply played the one winning card he did have... her undeniable desire for him.

It still appalled Sara that one rogue male could wreak that much havoc. Everything she'd thought she knew about herself had been ripped apart and put together again in a new arrangement that felt entirely alien... and all within the space of twenty-four hours. Little wonder that she had been guilty of such serious misjudgement; little wonder that she had been in turmoil, at the mercy of a seething sexual attraction which had betrayed her when she'd been desperate enough to seek any form of comfort.

'I knew you wouldn't tell tales...'

Sara spun from the low wall that separated the rambling garden from the fields. Antonia was standing a few feet away.

'Only because I didn't see that it would achieve anything but more distress all round.' Sara tilted her chin.

Antonia uttered a sharp little laugh. 'Brian won't even speak to me. He still thinks I made that phone call.'

'Of course you did,' Sara said drily, not having wasted one ounce of mental energy on that minor point.

'I didn't!' her cousin launched back at her furiously. 'I *didn't* make that call! Someone who knew about Brian and me obviously decided it would be fun to drop us in it! Maybe someone he works with, someone who saw us out together... I don't know... but it *wasn't* me!'

Sara didn't care who had made that call to the office. But she was grimly amused by her cousin's vociferous self-defence. Guilty of sleeping with Brian and guilty of complete absence of remorse, but not guilty of making that phone call.

'So tell me the true story about Alex Rossini,' Antonia demanded.

'Why?'

'I could do with a laugh to lighten my day,' Antonia derided. 'Ma has to be out of her mind to imagine that Alex would look at you twice, never mind take you home for the night! Alex Rossini wouldn't even give *me* the time of day the one time I met him. Why do you think I settled for Marco? I bet the most intimate thing you ever did for Alex Rossini was take dictation over breakfast!'

Sara turned back to the wall and braced her hands on the worn stone. She thought of all the years that she had wasted trying to make a friend of Antonia, wondered now why she had bothered when she had been beaten from the outset. Antonia had never forgiven her for depriving her of her cherished only-child status in her family home. Even though her cousin had effortlessly continued to bask in the limelight constantly shone on her by her besotted parents, Sara had remained a bitterly resented intruder.

When Sara had begun dating Brian, the pairing had been popular with both families. Brian's mother loathed Antonia, had been seriously worried when her son had shown an interest in her, and had been seriously relieved when, after a decent interval, he'd switched his interest to Sara instead. As for her uncle and aunt...they liked Brian but would have been very disappointed had their beautiful daughter settled for him. They expected Antonia to marry into wealth and status.

That Sara should get married first had rather astonished the Daltons. But her aunt had thoroughly enjoyed all the fuss of the wedding arrangements and over the past year Sara had grown closer to her than ever before. It hurt now to see that stronger bond broken and at such a cost to everyone concerned. Only Antonia, self-centred as ever, stood clear of the fallout. But then Antonia never took responsibility for anything she did.

'Why did you do it?' Sara asked now, not really expecting a response.

'Brian doesn't love you, he loves me...he just hasn't got the guts to admit it!' Antonia snapped, suddenly on the defensive.

Sara slowly turned, a frown of surprise etched between her brows.

'His mother hates me. She thinks I'm a tart. Brian does too... Why do you think he went for you? He wants me but he doesn't want me, so he played safe!'

Recognising the bitter resentment in Antonia's eyes, Sara was shaken. Ironically it had not occurred to her that her cousin might actually *care* about Brian. She had assumed that the entire episode had been yet another demonstration of Antonia's helpless need to smash anything which she herself valued. An act of spite and superiority.

'But there's only one thing I want to talk about,' Antonia continued angrily. 'Brian's acting like an idiot, chasing after you, refusing to have anything to do with me...but that's only because he's feeling guilty. Let him off the hook. Tell him you understand and that you accept that your engagement is over. I don't want him to feel trapped with me.'

'Trapped?' Sara echoed, not following.

Antonia looked unconvincingly coy and then shrugged a slim shoulder with quite unhidden self-satisfaction. 'I think I may be pregnant...'

'I think I may be pregnant...' It was like a body-blow to Sara. She went white. In an instant she learnt that her pain was not yet at an end. She had faced up squarely to their betrayal...but still the concept of Antonia pregnant with Brian's child could only make her feel sick. *She* had expected to have Brian's child.

'And I'm not telling him until he's stopped this stupid guilt trip about you!'

'I might as well have told tales...' Sara mumbled.

'No!' Antonia told her sharply. 'There's no reason for anyone to know *when* I got caught. You take yourself off back to London. I will be seen consoling Brian and then we'll go abroad and get hitched on a beach somewhere without any fuss. Everyone will think we were madly impulsive but I doubt if they'll suspect it was a shotgun do!'

'You have it all worked out.' No humiliation for Antonia.

'Brian was mine,' her cousin said with flat emphasis. 'And I can't say sorry when I don't feel sorry. Just you make sure you tell him I didn't make that phone call.'

A hysterical laugh clogged Sara's throat. Antonia didn't only expect her to take the heat for her, she also expected her to intercede on her behalf with Brian. So her cousin wasn't as sure of Brian as she wanted to be. But then why else would she be pregnant? That, given Antonia's experience, was unlikely to be an accident. Dear Lord, for how long had they been meeting behind her back?

In the kitchen Janice Dalton was fussing frantically over a tea-tray. 'Brian and his parents have come over!' she said, tight-mouthed. 'What are your uncle and I supposed to say to them?'

Sara almost laughed but she was afraid that if she did she wouldn't be able to stop. Brian here? And with his parents in tow? She had already heard all about how shocked and furious the Shorters were. Everyone was jumping on the same bandwagon. In the Dark Ages she'd have been dragged out to the village common and burnt as a witch for the sin of having offended so many people.

Be careful of what you wish for in case you get it . . . Last week she had passionately hated her dull, 'nice girl' image; this week she would have given ten years of her life to have her reputation back, to be able to walk down the village street again without nudges, turned backs and coldly disapproving stares. Notoriety wasn't fun, not in a small, close-knit community where so many people reserved the right to stand in moral judgement.

The doorbell shrilled. Halfway down the polished hall she was intercepted by Brian as he emerged from the lounge. 'Sara . . . I had to see you. We have to sort this out.'

'Tell them the truth!' she gasped, incredulous at his persistence and attempting to drag her arm free of his hold.

'Why did you tell your aunt we were finished? Why the blazes did you have to get caught in that stupid photo with Alex Rossini?' Brian demanded resentfully. 'Don't you realise what an idiot that's made me look? I know there's nothing going on between you and Rossini . . . there *couldn't* be...but it's made things even more complicated.'

The doorbell went again as if someone had a finger welded to the button. The piercing noise ground along her already jagged nerve-endings like a knife being sharpened.

'Let go of me,' Sara pleaded in despair, her voice shaking.

'I love you and I still want to marry you... If we don't talk, how are we going to work this out?'

Sara couldn't bear to listen to him. It was as if Brian was living in some fantasy world of his own. She tore herself free of his grasp with such force that she almost crashed against the front door. She hauled it open, her strained face a mask of desperation.

It was Alex. The shock of it rocked her back on her heels. But she experienced a flood of relief so powerful that it left her dizzy. She swayed, her head swimming. Strong arms reached out and caught her before her knees could buckle beneath her.

'What the hell has been going on here?' Alex demanded chillingly.

'Alex...' Sara whispered as she leant up against him, entirely supported by his superior strength and so grateful for his presence that she felt weak. 'Get me out of here...*please*!'

'Take your hands off her!' Brian raked at him after an astounded pause.

Alex ignored him. Swinging on his heel, he walked Sara out to a black Bugatti sports car, calmly slotted her into the passenger seat and murmured softly, 'I'll be back in a minute, *cara*.'

Sara snatched in an unsteady breath. Who do you think Alex is—some white knight riding gallantly to your rescue? a little voice asked drily. She shut the voice off. All she knew was that she had never been so glad to see anyone. At that moment it was more than enough.

She watched Alex emerge from the house again, couldn't even summon up the curiosity to wonder why he had gone back in. His black hair was ruffled by the breeze but so perfectly cut that it fell straight back into place. Dark eyes mirrored the sunlight—flashing gold against the hard symmetry of his masculine features. He looked quite extravagantly gorgeous in a pearl-grey suit that was very Italian in style. The overall effect was one of quite breathtaking elegance and sophistication. *Who* was she? she found herself wondering helplessly. Who was the woman who had walked away when Alex had laid his heart at her feet?

He swung in beside her. 'You have some preference about where you would like to go?'

'Anywhere...'

He laughed spontaneously. '*Dio*, I timed my arrival well. I also have plans of my own...'

That was scarcely a revelation. Alex would always know exactly where he was going and what he was doing. Unlike Brian...Brian, who she had once fondly believed to be strong, decisive and forthright, she reflected painfully. Right now Brian seemed lost in a turmoil of his own making, and he had been loyal to neither her nor Antonia. Had Brian come to her that day in her office and told her that he *loved* her cousin, she would have respected him more and understood him better.

'You've lost weight,' Alex remarked casually.

'Scarlet women do.'

'You get much thinner and you'll slide through a grating. There wasn't a lot of you to begin with.'

Was she getting too thin? She glanced down anxiously at the slender curves filling out her pink cotton T-shirt and jeans, and for some reason also recalled that she had no makeup on. Her cheeks flushed. For goodness' sake! It wasn't as if she was out on a hot date!

'Why did you come down?' she asked.

'I missed you?'

'Try again.'

'I was a little worried about the effect of all the publicity?'

'The little-office-girl-makes-good bit... or the Alex-Rossini-goes-down-market bit?'

'If being with you is slumming, there's not an office girl in the City safe.' Alex casually tossed a newspaper onto her lap. 'Have you seen the latest?'

Sara stiffened. 'I thought I'd had my fifteen minutes of fame.'

With a sinking heart, she read the gossip column. Tasmin Laslo was reportedly furious to learn that she had been replaced by a woman she described as 'an impertinent little typist', and the actress had gone on to share the news that the same typist had called her employer 'a slick, womanising swine'.

'I said it,' Sara whispered sickly. 'I said it that day when she phoned... that she was well rid of you.'

'Honesty got the better of you?'

'You have every right to be angry with me,' Sara conceded tautly.

'It was a fair assessment of my character to date. I don't give a damn, but if I know Tasmin she'll find a way to make this story run and run.'

Yet even in receipt of that daunting assurance Sara could feel a sense of calm stealing over her for the first time in days. It was the most incredible relief to escape the hothouse pressure and angry tensions of the Dalton household.

'Antonia's pregnant.' It leapt straight out of her subconscious onto her tongue.

Alex burst out laughing. Sara dealt him a stunned look.

'Sorry, *cara*. That was not very kind of me... but it does cross one's mind that, whatever else she is, she's a remarkably determined young woman.'

'Brian doesn't know yet. Of course, when he does... he'll leave me alone.'

'Is that what you want?'

'Yes . . . absolutely,' Sara returned, fiercely defensive on that point.

'I suspect the heat is already off you,' Alex delivered smoothly. 'When I went back into the house, I told them.'

Her seat belt pulled tight as Sara's back jerked blade-straight. 'Told them what?'

'I only wanted to make myself known to your family. Under fire, you surely did not expect me to pose alongside you as a martyred miscreant?'

Sara's jaw dropped as she gazed back at him wide-eyed. 'What did you tell them?'

'I merely pointed out that our relationship only began after you discovered that your fiancé and your cousin had been seeing each other behind your back. I was far kinder to them than they were to you,' Alex imparted, quite untouched by her consternation. 'I did not refer to the fact that you found them between the sheets. I find it quite impossible to comprehend why you should have felt the need to protect them in the face of the kind of treatment you have obviously been receiving.'

'It'll devastate my aunt and uncle—'

'Let them be devastated. She is their daughter and you are not her keeper.'

'You had no right to tell them!' Sara gasped.

'In the light of what I overheard before I entered the room, I enjoyed telling them. Your cousin staged a most unconvincing faint. Your ex put on a fetching impression of a trout on a hook. And then, as I was withdrawing to leave them all to it, the rather large blonde woman in the pearls made a decidedly offensive remark about your cousin's morals . . . something which rankled so severely that your cousin literally couldn't take it lying down.' Alex's accented drawl trembled with betraying amusement. 'She came up out of her faint like a vampire rising from the tomb and began screeching at the top of her voice!'

'Quite priceless entertainment, I gather?' But Sara's own voice had developed an involuntary wobble. She was genuinely shocked by Alex's sublime indifference to the feelings of everyone concerned but the picture that he had drawn was so vivid, so innately rich with black comedy that she couldn't help the ripple of amusement which briefly gripped her.

'You see, *bella mia* . . . you can laugh and smile again,' Alex murmured with satisfaction.

'Even when I hate myself for it? Even when I have no right to feel superior to Brian and Antonia?' she muttered feverishly. 'The same day. . . I slept with you.'

'But you would never have done that had you still considered yourself morally bound to him. You're too loyal. Nor can I believe that you would have practised such deceit as they did.'

'You could talk me right out of my conscience,' Sara whispered.

'It might be an improvement if you stopped behaving like a schoolgirl fresh out of a convent. Nobody's perfect,' Alex reminded her, taking some of the sting out of that initial statement.

'I owe Antonia's parents a great deal. If they hadn't given me a home when I was five, I would have gone into care. They took me in and brought me up just as if I was their own child.'

'Liar. I saw a dozen photos of her decorating the room, none whatsoever of you. They are comfortably off yet you left school at sixteen and made your own way in life.'

'My choice. You couldn't have expected them to do more. My aunt didn't even particularly want to take me on. I'm illegitimate,' Sara pointed out stiffly.

'Not so uncommon these days.'

'My father was a Greek waiter.'

'Rich, warm Mediterranean blood . . . do I apologise for mine?' Alex elevated an ebony brow with decided hauteur.

Sara was betrayed into a rueful laugh. 'I wasn't apologising—'

'You were. How did your parents meet?'

'My mother was on holiday. She was only out there a week. She was twenty-one,' Sara told him. 'Nobody wanted her to keep me but she did. So they told her she could manage on her own... It's fair enough that they weren't exactly over the moon when I landed back on their doorstep. My grandparents were too old to take me on. Antonia was only a year older. My aunt and uncle stepped in. They didn't *have* to.'

Alex made no comment. Sara rested her head back, the tension draining out of her, her limbs slowly sinking into relaxation. 'As usual I'm not asking where we're going.'

'You don't really care.'

Her skin reddened. 'No... I'm just grateful for a break.'

'I don't want gratitude, *cara*.'

An odd chill ran down her spine. As she watched the countryside flying by she never forgot for one moment that she was sitting beside Alex Rossini. Her awareness of him was so intense that she couldn't hide from it. The frozen front that she had once contrived to put up in his presence was now quite impossible to maintain.

'We're almost there.' Alex swung off the road and drove down a long, tree-lined lane past a Gothic gatehouse.

'Where is "there"?' She tested a smile, found it was not so difficult as she had imagined it would be.

'Ladymead Hall. It's on the market and I have an appointment to view it.'

'You want a house in the country?'

'A base within easy reach of London.' Alex brought the powerful car to an abrupt halt before it hit a string of potholes. There was already a Mercedes parked ahead of them.

Sara gazed out at the mellowed brick frontage of the Elizabethan manor house. Interest flickered and then slowly flamed. She climbed out. Sunlight glinted off the mullioned windows, several of which were boarded up. The ancient building had the same sad air of neglect as the overgrown grounds.

'Do you want me to wait in the car?' Sara asked abruptly across the bonnet.

'Of course not.' Alex strolled forward to greet the suavely suited estate agent, but Sara changed course and walked over to the entrance, not wishing to intrude.

'We'll explore alone.' Rejoining her, Alex planted a glossy brochure carelessly in her hand. 'You can give me the feminine viewpoint.'

The interior was better preserved than the exterior had suggested. The great hall had a massive stone fireplace and a wonderful flagstone floor. From room to room Sara wandered silently by Alex's side, her rapt face taking in the intact linenfold panelling, the elaborate if filthy plasterwork on the ceilings. The kitchen still rejoiced in massive built-in dressers. She pictured an Aga...a green one...in the fireplace. No, not there—that old black range ought to be cleaned up and preserved, she decided. The Aga would have to go at the other end.

A mouse ran over her foot; she didn't notice it. She roamed industriously through the maze of little dirty rooms which ran off the kitchen, mentally labelling them—logs, laundry, cloakroom, boiler room, junk—and frowned in intense concentration when she ran out of labels. She climbed the lavishly carved oak staircase, her fingers lingering here and there on the elaborate exuberance of the Jacobean ornamentation. Not a single word passed her lips.

Finally, at the head of the long gallery, sunlight beaming in from the windows in diamond patterns, dust motes dancing in the air, Sara uttered a dreamy sigh of enchantment and then endeavoured to be rationally judgemental for Alex's benefit. 'It's a very large house.'

'Do you think so? I thought it was rather modest,' Alex admitted softly.

Sara gazed out of a tall window and another smile curved her generous mouth. 'There's a topiary garden down there. I wonder if it could be saved? I suppose there once would have been a herb garden too.'

'An enormous amount of renovation would be required.'

Sara's head spun round, dismayed green eyes flying to him. 'You surely wouldn't let that put you off?'

'I have to confess that I would prefer to buy after someone else had done the dirty work.'

She thought of his immaculate Georgian house in London, the cool, contemporary decor of the few rooms that she had glimpsed, and nodded in rueful understanding.

'But I can see this as a family house...as a home,' Alex said, his accent feathering almost seductively over the syllables.

'Yes,' she sighed, thinking, Definitely not down Alex's street.

'Marry me and make it that...'

Her lashes flew up on stunned emerald eyes, her breath tripping in her throat. She stared back at him in a daze of disbelief.

'I want a wife, and...eventually...children.' Alex selected the last word with the same utterly complete calm. 'I also want you. We both appear to want the same things at this stage in our lives. Why should we not seek them together?'

The tip of her tongue stole out to moisten her full lower lip. Her mind was a total blank, and then she met Alex's dark golden gaze and the electrifying effect scorched along every nerve-ending, igniting a sudden surge of colour in her cheeks. She trembled, shattered by the immediacy of a response over which she had absolutely no control.

He took a prowling step closer. 'We already have the passion without which no marriage of convenience could hope to prosper. You want me, *bella mia* . . . do not be ashamed to admit that.'

'I can't believe that you want to get married—'

'I'm thirty-four, Sara...and I openly confess to having enjoyed my freedom for many years. However, women are not the only ones who get the urge to settle down with one partner.'

'I know but—'

'A practical marriage and a civilised relationship—that is what I am offering you. Where there is no strong emotion there will be no pain either,' Alex pointed out, his night-dark eyes skimming over her troubled face. 'In short, I will not hurt you, Sara.'

Alex didn't want a wife who was madly in love with him. He didn't want to become the focus of emotions that he had no intention of returning. That made a cold kind of sense to her. Women in love could be very demanding creatures. A woman in love with a man who did not love her might easily become jealous, possessive and insecure if the inequality within the relationship began to threaten her self-respect.

'Why me . . . for heavens' sake?' Sara murmured not quite steadily. 'You hardly know me.'

'I beg to differ. You have worked for me for a year. I know you to be cool under pressure, efficient, something of a perfectionist and an excellent organiser. You are more likely to be early for an appointment than late. You are respected and liked by your subordinates but regarded as rather reserved because you never participate in the office gossip.'

Sara was blushing fierily. 'I do hope you'll put all that in a reference for when I go job-hunting again. I sound like a model employee.'

'You were, but you were never ambitious in the career stakes.'

Sara turned away, her lower limbs feeling as if they were stuffed with cotton wool. 'No,' she conceded wryly.

'Which also suits my purposes. I travel a great deal. A wife with a demanding career of her own would have little time to spare for home and family in my absence.'

'Home and family'? Damn him, damn him, damn him for the calculating, coolly assured character assessor that he was! Alex knew what she had so lately lost, could only be aware of the strength of the lure that he was casting out to her when she was facing a wretchedly uncertain future, bereft of everything that she had expected to be hers.

'And, if you will forgive me for making the point, I believe I have also seen you at your worst.'

Her narrow back went rigid. 'Falling-down drunk and desperate?'

'You were still strong, still worthy of my respect...you threw no tantrums, wallowed in no self-pity and indulged in no vindictive outbursts. You behaved with remarkable self-restraint. I admired that.'

He had to be a lethal poker player. Sara had an insane image of herself going down on her knees and kissing his feet in gratitude for such assurances. But Alex *had* treated her with respect, consideration and understanding, without any overtones of superiority or pity. All those things Alex had given her and she had taken, not even truly valuing what she was receiving at the time.

Yet Brian, whom she had loved and trusted and believed in, had almost destroyed her. Brian...still talking about reconciliation with the arrogant and distasteful conviction that no matter what he had done she would ultimately forgive him. Brian, coolly disparaging her worth with his incredulity that a male of Alex's wealth and importance could find her deserving of interest. She had never seen that conceit and egotism in Brian until now.

There was a savage irony in making a comparison between two such radically different men, one whom she had adoringly placed on a pedestal and endowed with every conceivable virtue, the other whom she had disliked and misjudged and distrusted. She was ashamed of that now—ashamed that her gauche unease in Alex's disturbingly physical presence had led her into such unjustifiable prejudice.

'Alex . . . I can't deny that you're tempting me . . . but I don't think that I'm in a state of mind right now to be dealing with such a major decision,' Sara returned unsteadily, her jewel-like eyes unguarded and anxious.

'No doubt you feel that you don't know me well enough.'

'I know you well enough, Alex,' Sara said a little shyly, reflecting that while she had been at her worst Alex had been at his best. 'And the one thing this mess with Brian has taught me is that even though I've known him almost all my life I didn't *really* know him at all when the chips were down. I didn't suspect that he was still attracted to Antonia and I didn't once notice anything odd in his behaviour, but then, as you said, love makes you take people for granted, gives you a false, rosy picture and too many high-flown ideas. Was it like that for you— I mean with . . . ?'

'Elissa? Naturally. At that age I was a great romantic. But the pain fades . . . I can assure you of that,' he replied very drily.

Elissa—lovely name, she thought abstractedly as she gazed at Alex's chiselled golden profile. He was so very, very good-looking that even at a time like this, when it was so important that she should not be distracted, she was.

'You're a very rich man,' Sara pointed out in some embarrassment. 'There must be loads of women . . . you know . . . who would be much more suitable than me . . .'

Alex dealt her a cynically amused smile. 'But you are very special, *cara*. My embarrassment of riches did not tempt you an inch away from your moral standards last week. I liked that too. I would not like to be married solely on the basis of what I can deliver materially.'

It crossed her mind that Alex believed he had her so well taped that she would provide him with no unwelcome surprises. Perhaps all that she had despised in herself a mere week ago was ironically Alex's standard of what his wife should be. An old-fashioned homemaker with traditional values, highly unlikely to take off with the chauffeur one day, or announce that pregnancy might ruin her figure, or make spoilt-rich-girl demands on a male who was very much accustomed to having everything go *his* way.

'I don't know what to say...'

'You say yes.' Alex stretched out his hands and she reached for them, helplessly revelling in the warmth of physical contact.

'It would be crazy.'

'If you think that, my talents as a negotiator must be failing.'

Alex was a brilliant negotiator, pulling off the kind of stunning deals which made his competitors howl in anguish. But to negotiate a marriage proposal seemed so...so *cold*. Hurriedly she squashed the suspicion. There was nothing cold about the male arms relentlessly tugging her closer, nothing cold about utilising intelligence and cool, calm forethought in so important a field as choosing a life partner, she told herself.

'I can't think straight...'

He laughed softly, dark eyes flashing gold with innate male satisfaction. He knew why she was in such a condition, knew that he could draw her, unresisting and quivering, into contact with every hard, muscular line of his length and extract a response that she had not yet learned to control.

With a shapely hand he stroked a silky strand of black hair back from her brow. Her heartbeat was racing like crazy, her breasts lifting within a light cotton bra which suddenly felt unbearably restrictive. 'I also like the fact that I excite you...' Alex purred.

A flush of horribly self-conscious heat marked out her slanted cheekbones as he glanced down at the thrusting evidence of her stiffened nipples poking through the cotton jersey. 'Don't be shy,' he reproved her, leaning her back against the wall, sliding his hands below the T-shirt to skim caressingly up over the smooth skin of her taut ribcage.

Sara stopped breathing, held still by the smoulder of his golden eyes. With breathtaking cool, he flipped the bra out of his path. Her breasts sprang full and heavy into his shaping hands. Sensation fired a bitter-sweet ache between her thighs. She trembled. His thumbs grazed the achingly sensitive buds and she moaned and jerked, looking down at her wantonly bare flesh in mingled disbelief and excitement.

His dark head lowered. He ran the tip of his tongue along her full lower lip and then, with innately erotic precision, intruded sexily into the moist interior already invitingly opened to him. A stifled moan was torn from her, her hands rising of their own volition and clutching at his shoulders to prevent her sliding down the wall in an inelegant heap of shuddering responsiveness.

'If you don't become my wife, I'll make you my mistress,' Alex warned softly. 'I am not going to go away, not about to politely withdraw in gentlemanly defeat.'

He straightened, expertly replaced her disarranged clothing. Sara was shaking but not so controlled by the dissastisfied ache of her shamefully willing body that she was deaf to the message he wanted her to receive. Angry humiliation leapt up in place of passion. She stepped back and flung him a look of warning. 'If you ever do that to me again, Alex, I'll slap your face—hard! I am not some brainless little toy you can play with and I'm not a wind-up doll either. I will not be controlled or manipulated by you!'

'But you will marry me.'

The conviction with which he made that assurance threw Sara even further off balance.

'I . . . I need to think about it,' she muttered unevenly.

'Back in that madhouse? How could you think there? I want an answer now,' Alex declared. 'Yes or no will suffice . . . for this round.'

She wrenched her eyes from him, struggled to rise above the quite startling temptation to tell him to take his proposal and jump off a cliff. Her brain told her that she was too emotionally charged up right now to make a level-headed decision but every other natural prompting urged blind, immediate acceptance.

Alex was offering her everything that she had ever wanted on terms that she could fulfil, and on one level there was a part of her, which she tried and failed to overcome, that was helplessly, deeply influenced by the knowledge that Alex wanted her and valued her. That awareness was balm to her salvaged ego and Alex was offering her an unbelievably welcome escape from a situation that was threatening to become quite intolerable.

'Yes.' The instant she said it she almost retracted it again, but then she thought of how it would feel to stand on the sidelines while Antonia married Brian. She would be an object of pity, the spectre at the feast, the on-looker who embarrassed everyone. In one small family there was no room for the rejected bride *and* her replacement. Why put herself through such humiliation? Nobody could possibly feel sorry for Alex Rossini's chosen wife . . . could they?

CHAPTER FIVE

'IT'S a magnificent gown. Of course we couldn't have afforded anything this elaborate,' Janice Dalton remarked stiffly. 'I expect with the number of important people coming Alex wanted you to look really special. But your uncle and I will feel total frauds sitting at the top table. We haven't done a thing to help... But then it's all been done in such a frantic rush...'

Sara sent the older woman a veiled glance, troubled by her constrained manner. Alex's revelation about Antonia and Brian had shattered her aunt. Both the Daltons had been very upset by their daughter's behaviour. Brian and Antonia's deceit had been a bitter pill to swallow, unsweetened by Antonia's refusal to express the slightest regret.

'Sara... it's still not too late to change your mind,' her aunt muttered tightly.

The wedding was a mere two hours away. Sara almost laughed at the idea. 'I don't want to change my mind.'

'Alex is very rich and very handsome,' the older woman added with a rather peevish edge to her delivery. 'But he's also a rather overwhelming personality. Naturally, I want you to be happy... but are you really sure you're making the right decision?'

'I want to marry Alex.' That belief had buoyed Sara up over every day of the past month. It was like a rock that she clung to when the winds of change threatened to howl around her. As long as she had focused on Alex, her future home and her approaching wedding, she had been able to sit safe inside a neat little emotional cocoon. Brian and Antonia had gone back to London. She had seen neither of them since that day when Alex had swept her off in the Bugatti to Ladymead. Both her cousin and her ex-fiancé had found retreat from family recrimina-tions the most comfortable option.

Ladymead... An abstracted smile curved Sara's lips. Alex had bought her dream house. He had sent her back to the car with the satirical assurance that he didn't want the estate agent to catch one glimpse of her enchanted face. 'Do you know if there's anybody else interested?' she had pressed anxiously.

'There is precious little that I desire that I cannot buy.' For an instant, assailed by the dryness of that tone and the sudden coolness of those brilliant dark eyes, Sara had experienced the most peculiar inner chill.

She shook off the memory, choosing to recall instead her aunt and uncle's shaken response to Alex's an-nouncement that same evening that they were getting married as soon as it could be arranged. 'A rather over-whelming personality'... Yes, the Daltons had been so overpowered by Alex that they hadn't uttered a word of protest, had indeed struggled valiantly to conceal their astonishment, but there had also been perceptible relief in their reaction. If Sara had found another bride-groom, nobody needed to feel quite so bad.

Alex had assured them that he would handle all the arrangements. And he had...or his staff had. Sara hadn't had an input either and hadn't wanted one. She had spent the past year up to her throat and revelling in all the endless tiny details of bridal fervour. This time she was grateful not to be involved, not to be reminded of that *other* wedding which would now never take place. Alex had been supremely tactful, she thought gratefully.

The doorbell went. Her aunt went downstairs. Sara frowned when she heard her uncle Hugh's voice. He sounded upset. She walked out onto the landing.

'Tell me it isn't true,' her uncle was protesting dazedly.

'You can't make an announcement like that on Sara's wedding day!' her aunt was saying vehemently to someone standing out of view in the hall below. 'What would people think of you?'

'What's going on?' Sara asked tautly.

Antonia strolled forward and looked up. 'Brian and I got married in a register office yesterday.'

Sara went very still. 'Congratulations,' she murmured. 'I am very pleased for you both.'

Ignoring the burst of angry speech from her uncle, Sara walked back into her bedroom. Well, she had known it was coming, hadn't she? And she was marrying Alex in a couple of hours. The bridesmaids, whom she had not even met, would be arriving soon— Alex's three half-sisters, all flown in from abroad for the occasion and putting up at the Savoy. Her eyes burned. She quivered, drew in a deep breath and slowly let it escape again. She even contrived a wry smile. Antonia had, as usual, beaten her to the starting line. And she did wish them happy. It was just...just that she would rather not have known today...that was all.

'You and Alex Rossini...'

Sara jerked around. She hadn't heard the door open. Antonia stood on the threshold, her eyes glittering feverishly beneath the stylish brimmed hat she wore.

'Please don't cause a scene,' Janice Dalton pleaded tautly, preceding her daughter into the room.

'Sara makes me sick,' Antonia hissed rawly, ignoring her mother. 'Always says the right thing, always does the right thing. And—whoopee—she grabs a billionaire the same day she loses Brian! I bet Alex Rossini is madly in love with her too...he certainly can't wait to get her to the altar! I bet her mother-in-law adores her just like that old witch Shorter does! I bet she's going to spend the rest of her life in the lap of luxury, cosseted and appreciated and adored. It would make *anyone* want to throw up!'

And with that bitterly resentful conclusion Antonia stalked out again. The only sound that broke the thrumming silence was the thunderous slam of the front door.

Tight-mouthed, Sara's aunt sank into a chair. 'She's so horribly jealous of you. She always was...'

Jealous? Antonia jealous of *her*? Sara was stunned by the concept.

'We spoilt her more when we saw how she felt. We thought that would make her feel more secure. But it didn't change her feelings and it really isn't her fault, you know,' the older woman continued defensively. 'After all, she wasn't asked for her opinion when we took you into the family.'

'I can't believe Antonia could be jealous of me.'

Her aunt gave her a humourless smile. 'Of course she's jealous, Sara. People always seem to like you more than they like her. Other women are envious of her looks and can't bear the competition. All too many people are willing to judge Antonia for becoming involved with Brian...when really it's something that could have happened to anyone. But that's why I've invited them both to your wedding.'

Sara slowly turned from the mirror. 'You invited *them*...you invited Brian?' she whispered sickly, belatedly understanding the significance of Antonia's very dressy outfit.

Her aunt lifted her greying head high. 'I thought it would look better if they both came. It will show our friends that there's no acrimony, just a rather last-minute change of partners.' Her voice hardened. 'I don't want people thinking badly of my daughter, Sara.'

'No.' Sara understood that, but, while she could have borne Antonia out of respect to her uncle and aunt, she *still* didn't want Brian at her wedding.

The arrival of Alex's sisters in their finery was a very welcome diversion. Sara had not yet fathomed the complex Rossini family tree that was the result of Alex's father currently being on his fifth wife. Alex's mother had been Sandro Rossini's first wife and the only one to pass on into history through death rather than divorce. Donatella and the identical twins, Cara and Lucilla, all crowded into Sara's far from large bedroom, bubbling with curiosity, excitement and mercifully excellent English.

'So like Alex to do the unexpected,' Donatella laughed, and spontaneously grasped Sara's hands. An attractive brunette, she was only a couple of years younger than Alex, still single and a water-colour artist of growing reputation in Italy. 'I would kiss you but I might smudge your make-up.'

'You're so beautiful!' Cara carolled with a fourteen-year-old's exuberance. 'I'm not surprised it took Alex a whole year to catch you! Papà is so relieved he's getting married at last. He thought Alex was never going to get over Elissa!'

'Let me help you with your gown.' Donatella stepped into the breach of sudden silence with easy tact while Lucilla nudged her twin in the ribs. Cara's cheeks were already burning fierily.

Elissa, blasted Elissa being mentioned *again*! Sara was astonished by the amount of annoyance running through her. For heaven's sake, Alex hadn't laid eyes on the wretched woman for thirteen years! Surely even the most passionate youthful love affair was little more than a sentimental memory after that length of time?

An hour later Sara walked up the aisle of the local church on her uncle's arm. Alex turned and dealt her a slow smile. Her nervous tension evaporated but her sense of unreality somehow increased. So many strange faces, so few familiar in the crowds that surrounded them while the photos were being taken after the ceremony. She watched security guards keeping the Press at bay. One of them looked eerily familiar, a premature and very noticeable streak of grey evident in his otherwise black hair... Where had she seen him before? The question nagged annoyingly at the back of her mind.

Alex's father, Sandro, embraced her with flattering enthusiasm. His six-foot-tall blonde wife, Francine, gave her an easy smile and shook hands. 'Welcome to the family, Sara,' she murmured in her distinctive American drawl.

As the limousine drew away from the church, Alex angled a wry glance at her. 'So we are finally together. Believe me, it wasn't my intention that we should scarcely see each other before the wedding. But the trips to New York and Milan were scheduled weeks ago.'

'I kept myself busy.' Sara hurried to assure him, keen to make him believe that she had not felt neglected and that she wasn't the type to moan and nag when business took him abroad. But in truth, she acknowledged, she had been thoroughly fed up. Two evenings out in three weeks, one of which had had to include her aunt and uncle, had done little to remove the lowering suspicion that once Alex had gained her agreement to marry him he had switched his entire attention back to more important things...like making more money, when he already had so much that he couldn't spend it in a lifetime!

'Yes. I understand you've been over at Ladymead on a very regular basis—'

'I wanted to be present when the surveys were being done, and that architect you recommended was marvellously helpful,' Sara responded with enthusiasm. 'And you remember that specialist I mentioned...?'

'Which one?' Alex enquired with a lack of interest so profound that even Sara could not have missed it.

Sara reddened. 'Sorry, am I being a bore?'

'You've kept me fully up to date with developments on the phone,' Alex reminded her with a rather grim smile.

'You do *like* Ladymead?' It shook Sara at that instant to recognise the fact that she had never asked Alex that question before.

'What a foolish question, *cara*. Of course I do.' He reached out and linked her taut fingers with his. 'You make a ravishing bride.'

'It's a gorgeous dress—'

'Don't do that...don't put yourself down. I would not have married a less than ravishingly beautiful woman,' Alex informed her with lazy mockery.

Much of the tension that he had awakened evaporated. Had she imagined that shadow darkening his lean features? She reminded herself that Alex was volatile and that, whether she liked it or not, she had to learn not to be over-sensitive to his fairly rapid changes in mood. And since she had always been the calm type, surely that wouldn't be too difficult?

'Antonia and Brian got married yesterday,' she told him tautly, wondering if her cousin and her ex would show up at the reception. She hadn't seen them at the church but then it was perfectly possible that she could have missed them in the crush.

'I hope it was as hole-and-corner as the courtship,' Alex said very drily.

'My aunt invited them both to the wedding.'

Alex withdrew his hand with a jerk and turned shimmering dark eyes on her. 'She did *what*?'

'Antonia *is* their daughter, Alex,' Sara pointed out ruefully. 'And my aunt felt that it would cause more comment if they weren't invited as a couple. Brian's mother has already been saying some very nasty things about Antonia to anyone prepared to listen—'

'When are *you* going to say them? *Dio*...love thy enemy,' Alex grated with impatience. 'I didn't want either of them present today.'

'I can understand why *I* could feel that way...but not why you should.' In the back of her mind loomed the horrid realisation that within an hour of the wedding they were having their first fight. 'After all, Brian is going to be like my brother-in-law now.' And her voice fractured slightly on that daunting realisation.

Alex treated her to a sizzling glance. 'Finding it difficult to adjust?'

Sara studied the hands now knotted on her lap. 'No... but I only heard an hour before I left the house this morning. I'm getting used to the idea already—'

'But not quick enough, *cara*,' Alex breathed with chilling bite. 'Not quick enough.'

That chill went right down inside her and hurt, making her feel rejected and shut out. She had been inexcusably tactless, she told herself angrily. Naturally Alex did not want to hear about Brian on their wedding day. Why hadn't she kept her stupid mouth shut? she asked herself as she slid out of the limo outside the fabulous country hotel where the reception was being staged.

'Much better than two million... you're a girl after my own heart,' Marco teased her as he kissed her on the cheek. 'No hard feelings?'

'No more cracks about boots and berries, little brother,' Alex interposed, making Marco flush.

'I'm not about to take my life in my hands.'

Pete drew her to one side, his anxious eyes meeting hers. 'You didn't tell Alex all that nonsense I spouted that morning, did you?' he prompted worriedly.

'Of course not.'

'I mean, *obviously*,' Pete stressed with an amused shake of his head as he perceptibly relaxed, 'Alex is nuts about you! I was way out of line.'

No, Pete hadn't been as far out of line as he fondly imagined, Sara found herself thinking irritably. She was a bit fed up with people saying how madly in love Alex was with her when it was so patently obvious that he was not. Oh, yes, he might be behaving as any bridegroom was expected to behave, but Sara knew that he was only putting on a good show. Why advertise the fact that this was a marriage of convenience? That was private, not for public consumption.

Five minutes before the meal began, Sara saw Antonia and Brian slipping into the only two seats left vacant. Her cousin was wearing a fixed smile. By her side Brian looked grim and uncomfortable. Nothing could have concealed the marks of strain that had thinned his face and lent a harsher line to his mouth.

'The happy twosome,' Alex commented flatly. 'They deserve each other, don't you think?'

Sara focused on her wineglass. 'I wish them well. I really do.'

'If you tell yourself that often enough, I might actually start to believe it too,' Alex breathed with an undertone of rawness that sent her tension screaming up another notch.

After the meal Alex whirled her round the dance-floor with breathtaking expertise. It was Sara who mumbled apologies when she collided with his feet and who couldn't wait to sit down again because she felt that her lack of dexterity, her sheer clumsiness must be embarrassing him when every eye in the room was upon them.

A little while later she was chatting to family friends when she felt a hand touch her shoulder. She turned her head with an enquiring smile. She had to force the smile to stay in place when she saw Brian.

'Care to dance?' he asked loudly.

Sara hesitated, alarmingly conscious of their audience. 'If you like,' she said grudgingly.

'Antonia was determined to come, so don't blame me,' Brian muttered in an embittered undertone as he pulled her onto the floor. 'Dear God, Sara...what happened to us?'

'You know exactly what happened, Brian.'

'But I feel like some bloody pawn people push around for fun!' he vented down at her, his face furiously flushed. 'I was set up, Sara. Last week I found out that some private investigator had been snooping around after me, pestering my colleagues at work, blasted well paying for information about my movements!'

Sara wondered uneasily if he was drunk. 'A private investigator?' she queried, incredulous at the suggestion as they proceeded round the floor at the snail's pace of the vaguely dancing shuffle which had always been their style.

'You tell me how anyone knew Antonia and I were going to be in the flat that day at that time. It was a last-minute arrangement. And who made that phone call which brought you there to find us *in flagrante delicto*?' he completed bitterly.

Her mouth compressed. 'I really don't see that it matters now—'

'The only person I know who could afford a private investigator is your new husband!' Brian cut in with clenched teeth. 'He's rich, he's devious and he hates me like poison, and if you ask me I'm lucky I'm still alive! Back in his homeland that smooth, calculating bastard would probably just have hired a hit man to get me out of the way!'

'Have you any idea how ridiculous you sound?' Sara enquired in disbelief, tugging back from him because anger was making him grip her far too tightly and closely for comfort. 'Why should Alex have hired a private investigator?'

'Well, you ask yourself who got what he most wanted out of this nightmare. And Rossini must have wanted you very badly to marry you this quickly! Very neat, wasn't it—how he was in the right place at the right time to step into my shoes...not off abroad the way he usually is, not involved with another woman... No, he was right there waiting to catch you on the rebound, wasn't he?'

'Forgive me for interrupting this touching reunion...'

Alex's smoothly controlled drawl sent a shiver down Sara's taut spinal cord as her head whipped round in shock. She had never heard that much menace, wasn't surprised when Brian paled and abruptly dropped his arms from her. 'Hates me like poison', Brian had said, and it occurred to her that that bit was certainly true.

Bypassing Brian, Alex drew her close, his strong face tight with suppressed anger.

Sara stumbled and said, 'Why do you dislike him so much?'

'He's still breathing, walking around, causing trouble.'

An uneasy laugh was torn from her. 'Alex...he wasn't trying to make a pass at me.'

'Were you hoping he would? Or was it enough of a power play merely to let his wife watch the two of you clinging to each other and so totally absorbed that neither of you noticed that the music had stopped?' Alex demanded with roughened quietness, dark eyes icy with condemnation.

Sara paled under the unexpected attack. 'It wasn't like that—'

'He's still in love with you... or at least he *thinks* he is, but he's married to another woman now. Your behaviour was inappropriate,' Alex spelt out grimly. 'As was his. But it is you whom I choose to censure, for you are my wife and I expect certain standards to be maintained, particularly in public. If you cannot maintain those standards around your former fiancé, how can you possibly remain in contact with your family? There will be no ongoing problems in that department, *cara*. I assure you of that.'

Sara was shaken and angered by his rebuke. In all her life she could not recall any male ever telling her that her behaviour had been unacceptable. Her pride smarted furiously. Possibly she should have been more distant with Brian in so public a setting when all too many people were aware of how recently their relationship had been severed, but she did not feel that she deserved to be dragged mortifyingly over the coals of Alex's grim disapproval as if she were a child who had let herself down in front of the grown-ups!

'If you had heard what Brian was saying, you might have understood why I was still standing there after the music had finished!' Sara returned defensively.

'You couldn't tear yourself away from him?'

She bridled. 'No, only not for the reasons you imagine. I couldn't believe what he was saying! Brian was accusing you of having put a private investigator on him, of having set him up to be caught in the act with Antonia...for h-heaven's sake...' As she noticed the sudden narrowing of Alex's dark gaze, his immediate, poised stillness, her voice tripped and then slowly drained away.

She had expected him to laugh with that wonderful spontaneity of his, or at worst react with angry exasperation at such an absurd allegation. But Alex did neither. His chiselled golden features clenched, his expressive mouth flattening, and then, in that pulsing silence, one of his twin sisters bounced in between them and grabbed his hand. Throwing Sara a mischievous glance, she tugged her big brother back onto the dance-floor.

As Sara hovered with an uncertain frown pleating her brows, she saw the man with the grey streak in his hair bending down to speak to Sandro Rossini. And it came to her then where she had seen that man before. Outside the flat that day when she had been fleeing from the sight of Brian and Antonia in each other's arms. Yet he was one of Alex's security guards. Maybe he lived in the same street. Coincidence, nothing more... How could it be anything more?

Alex couldn't *possibly* have had any connection with that episode. The very idea was ridiculous! Was Brian's paranoia contagious? But when had she ever known Brian to be paranoiac? Or Alex silent?

An image swam back up in her memory. She remembered Alex coming into her office that afternoon, not a single word of criticism passing his lips about the unanswered phones, his uncharacteristic quietness, his astonishing inability to distinguish between brandy and black coffee in spite of the fact that the bottle had been sitting in open view on Pete's desk... And even if he hadn't noticed all that he must surely have known that she was sloshed out of her stupid mind when she couldn't even walk in a straight line down the corridor!

The more likely scenario would have run very differently. Alex would have demanded to know why she wasn't answering the phones, seen the brandy bottle at one glance and incredulously insisted on an explanation. And only then did she recall the minor fact which she had forgotten in all the excitement. Alex *should* have been flying to Rome that afternoon...but he hadn't gone anywhere. Another coincidence?

With his sisters fussing around her, Sara went to change out of her wedding gown. How had Alex known that Brian was a salesman? That she lived with her cousin? Alex had known *too* much. And what about the dinner party he had mentioned, the keys of the company apartment right there in his pocket so that he could offer them without delay? Her heartbeat was pounding so loudly that it felt as though it was sitting at the foot of her throat. Smooth, slick womaniser...

'No woman would forgive such a betrayal...'

'How could you ever trust him again...?'

What she was imagining was sheer madness, she told herself weakly, but she could not forget Alex's silence. He had neither laughed nor defended himself. His impassivity had challenged her disbelief, indeed openly invited her suspicions...

Sheathed in an elegant suit in cream and black and showered in confetti, she slid breathlessly into the limousine that was to take them to the airport.

'Alex...' Sara licked uneasily at her dry lower lip. 'I'm about to ask you what is probably a very stupid question.'

'The investigator?'

Sara tried and failed to swallow, her intensely green eyes snapping to his diamond-sharp dark gaze.

'Guilty as charged. Yes...I put an investigator on him.'

'Y-yes?' Sara felt as if her voice was fighting through layers of concrete to be heard. To have had her wild suspicion flatly, unemotionally confirmed without the smallest preamble sent shock rolling over her in thunderous waves.

'I wanted you a great deal, Sara.'

'You set an investigator on Brian?' she whispered shakily, her flesh clammy.

'And his liaison with your cousin was duly discovered. I will be very frank; my initial intent was simply to tell you that he was having an affair.'

'Was it?' she asked stupidly.

'But the kill-the-messenger principle, allied with the fear that you might well disbelieve me, convinced me that such a direct approach would be unwise. Nor was our working relationship conducive to the delivery of such a very personal revelation,' Alex spelt out levelly. 'Sadly, it was necessary that you should discover them with your own eyes.'

'S-sadly?' Sara quavered, her entire attention nailed to him with a kind of sick fascination.

'I did not know that you would surprise them in bed,' Alex continued reflectively. 'I could hardly have arranged that.'

'But it was remarkably likely, wasn't it?' Sara's voice wobbled again. 'The phone call?'

'I arranged—'

'The security guard who works for you? I saw him in the street outside the flat.'

'A precaution for your safety...' Alex was beginning to sound very slightly defensive, as if her attitude was not quite what he had envisaged. 'I knew you might be upset—'

'*Might be*?' Sara stressed in agonised disbelief.

'I wanted to know where you were, what you were doing and that you were safe from any harm. I felt responsible for you.'

Her whole image of Alex shattered there and then. Brick by brick it fell apart, and then even the bricks crumbled to dust. She trembled in the face of the enormity of what he'd confessed with such incredible cool. He had set her up for the worst ordeal of her life and then calmly strolled in to play the good Samaritan and *plunder* what was left with the innate deviousness of a born manipulator. Sara was absolutely devastated.

'Sara... you had a right to know about their affair.'

'That's what reporters say when they rip someone's life apart for the public's entertainment—a right to know,' she repeated unevenly.

'As events swiftly proved, you would have found out anyway,' Alex reminded her grimly. 'Your cousin is pregnant. She was not about to stand idly by and watch you marry the father of her child.'

'That doesn't matter.' Numbly she moved her head to stress that negative response. She could feel the agony of betrayal threatening to smash a composure that consisted purely of shock. It was her second betrayal, her second acquaintance with the weakness of her own judgement in the space of a month. She had *trusted* Alex, and without that trust what was there?

'You played God with my life...' Sara shuddered at the awareness, suddenly understanding why Brian had said that he felt like a pawn. To have been manipulated to such a degree was intolerable. It made her feel supersmall and powerless and unbelievably dumb. But what savaged her most of all was the reality that she had so blindly put Alex on a pedestal too, trusting him, listening to him, feeling grateful that he was so tolerant and sympathetic that ghastly day. Now she saw everything she had felt, everything she had thought since about Alex as suspect and unreal.

'I did intend to tell you the truth eventually.'

'Maybe never.'

'Sara... he didn't deserve you.'

'And you did? Heaven knows, you must have got some kick out of playing the concerned employer for the first time in your wretched, self-centred life!' Sara condemned. 'And it was all a sham, Alex. None of it was real!'

'My sympathy and my concern were.'

'Like hell they were!' Sara snapped, feeling the acrid scorch of tears hitting the back of her eyes. 'You must have been delighted at how wonderfully it all went to plan! I even came back to the office to make it easier for you...I got drunk, I fell into your hands like an overripe plum, didn't I?' Her trembling voice broke right down the middle and she turned her head away sharply, forcing her vocal cords to do her bidding again. 'I hate you now...I'll never forgive you for this!'

At the airport she climbed out of the limousine on wobbling legs, fighting the tears off like mad. She, who never, ever cried, wanted to throw herself down in a humiliating heap and sob like a hysteric! When Alex dared to reach for her hand, she jerked away and discovered that in addition to crying she wanted to physically attack him. Never before in her life had she experienced such violent rage. So nobody was perfect...? Well, Alex hadn't touched the tip of the iceberg when he'd said that!

The instant the Rossini private jet was airborne Sara removed her seat belt and headed for the rear cabin. Alex followed her, his strong features taut. 'We have to talk—'

'Brian said that too and I should have bloody listened, shouldn't I?' Sara flung at him in her distress. 'Maybe he had his suspicions then, maybe we could have worked out that there was an *agent provocateur* involved.'

'It's a little late now...we're married.'

'And that certainly wasn't part of the original game plan, was it?' Sara accused him painfully, her head pounding fit to burst. 'You intended to catch me on the rebound and talk me into bed...but I even did that for you, didn't I? I dragged *you* into bed the same day!'

'Sara, don't...It wasn't like that.'

'I know what it was like...I was there!' Sara threw back rawly. 'You were prepared to wreck my future with the man I loved just for the sake of some sordid little fling! And if I had been stupid enough to agree to that I would now be clutching twenty-four red roses and a diamond bracelet! Another Alex Rossini cast-off to be sniggered at by the gutter press!'

'I asked you to marry me,' Alex gritted, a dark flush highlighting his slashing cheekbones.

'Wow, I'm such a lucky girl! I've landed myself a real hero. You're treacherous and dishonest and the only reason you proposed marriage was because it finally sunk in on that boundless ego of yours that that was the only way you were going to get me!'

'If we are to stoop to that level,' Alex drawled with a flash of white teeth and blazing golden eyes, 'I would remind you that when I proposed I had already had that particular pleasure.'

Sara went white and spun clumsily away from him. The reminder outraged her. She needed to hit back so badly that she was burning up inside. 'Well, you didn't get such a great bargain... a wife who's still hopelessly in love with another man! Maybe that makes us about equal,' she taunted bitterly out of savaged pride.

But the soft click of the door shutting on his exit was her only reply. A sob of stifled distress abruptly broke from Sara's compressed lips, and then another. She flung herself on the built-in bed and pushed her convulsing face into the softness of a pillow. Torn in two by the violence of her emotions, she let the tears flow because for the first time in many years of unyielding self-discipline she couldn't hold them back. In any case, there was no Antonia here now to sneer and laugh at such pathetic weakness.

How could Alex have done that to her? How could he have coolly admitted to such vile and inexcusable interference? Didn't he realise that this totally smashed the fragile foundations of their relationship? That there was nothing left—nothing but hatred and resentment and bitter regret inside her now.

CHAPTER SIX

UNFAMILIAR sounds woke Sara by degrees: quick, firm footsteps, the chiming clink of glass and china, then the swish of heavy curtains slowly being drawn back. Sunlight warmed her drowsy face and she opened her eyes.

'*Buon giorno, signora.*' A middle-aged woman was extending a satin and lace wrap to her with a smile.

Sara, sitting up with a start, found herself deftly enveloped in the garment. The pillows were plumped and a tray set before her. Venice ... She was in Venice in the magnificent *palazzo* which had been in the Rossini family for centuries. They had arrived very late last night to be greeted by the housekeeper, Marcella. Declining the offer of supper, Sara had been shown up to this exquisitely furnished room, so exhausted that it had been an effort to spare her fabulously ornate surroundings more than a dull-eyed glance. As she glanced at her watch now she realised in astonishment that she had slept the morning away.

Only when the bustling Marcella skimmed curious dark eyes across the pristine white pillow beside hers did Sara recall that last night had been her wedding night. Her creamy skin reddened with sudden embarrassment. It was perfectly obvious that she had spent the night alone and undisturbed. Why on earth should she be blushing over the fact? she asked herself furiously.

Yet she *had* somehow still expected to wake up with Alex beside her. The discovery of that inexplicable conviction infuriated her even more. Why on earth should she have expected that? She could only be grateful that Alex had accepted the reality that nothing would persuade her to share a bed with him now! After all, she had maintained a frigid silence from the instant the jet had landed, speaking only when forced to do so, making her hostility pointedly obvious. So why did the memory of that mute response in the face of his teeth-clenchingly perfect manners now make her squirm?

Some ten minutes later, still savouring the last bite of the delicious light meal she had eaten, Sara thrust away the tray and sprang out of bed. The skyline beyond the windows was a visual feast of domes, pinnacles, oddly shaped chimneys and campaniles. The Grand Canal below was as busy as any city highway at rush hour but the traffic was far more interesting. A speedboat foamed past, followed at a more sedate pace by a chugging *vaporetti* crammed to capacity and then a little barge heaped with vegetable produce, tailed by an old-fashioned fishing boat. Sara couldn't help being charmed by the sheer colourful vivacity of the scene.

In the adjoining bathroom she sank into a sumptuous sunken bath so large that it reminded her of a miniature swimming pool. But even such sybaritic splendour couldn't make her relax. She had rushed into marriage at breakneck speed. Who was to say that she hadn't asked for what she got? Who was to say that she didn't thoroughly deserve the mess she was now in? No such thing as a perfect hero, Sara, she told herself. But a male with a scruple or two—had that been too much to hope for?

Alex had no regrets either. Why should he care how it felt to be forced to see oneself as a purely sexual object . . . a female *thing*, desired for her body and for nothing else? For when you stripped all the pretences away that was the true sum of her worth to Alex. He had used all the right buzzwords like 'home' and 'family', blinding her with specious flattery and clever argument, but ultimately his sole objective had been her voluntary placing of her physical self into the bed of his choosing.

With her in love with another man and mere weeks from her wedding, the average male would have seen her as out of reach. But Alex lived in the rarefied society of the very rich, where anything could be acquired for the right price...or the right tactics. And Alex was famous for being so tortuously serpentine in his business negotiations and so innately secretive that even his top executives could be surprised, red-faced and drop-jawed when he pulled off some deal entirely on his own.

'You never really know what Alex is up to. It fairly keeps you on your toes,' Pete had grumbled once.

The decision to expose Brian's infidelity had cost Alex not one sleepless night. Shrewdly flicking through his options, Alex had known that nothing could better a first-hand encounter with her fiancé's feet of clay. And in one chillingly precise move he had ensured that her engagement would be broken so that he could smoothly step into the breach to persuade her that *he* was the 'far more entertaining possibility' that her future could offer.

Whatever else Alex was he was ruthless, aggressively resourceful and he thrived on challenge. Only what you saw was not necessarily what you got with Alex Rossini, she conceded painfully. Like some science-fiction shapeshifter, Alex could fit himself to any required backdrop, so that within a head-spinning handful of days Sara had been treated to Alex the reformed womaniser, hearing the pure clarion call of domesticity, talking about *settling down*, Alex the family man... Tears stung Sara's embittered eyes. Well, they said that there was a fool born every minute. She had swallowed every lying word whole!

'Did you sleep well?'

Dredged from her all-absorbing thoughts with a vengeance, Sara flinched in horror before she abruptly catapulted upright in a wave of noisily displaced water and snatched at a towel to shield her dripping length from the brazen male poised scant feet from her. Wide-eyed with disbelief, she clutched frantically at the towel and gaped at him. 'How dare you?' she shrilled.

An ebony brow was elevated. 'How dare I what?'

'Invade my privacy!' Sara gasped, hotly flushed as she struggled to anchor the fleecy towel round her, but the foot of it had already trailed in the water and the sodden weight of fabric was anything but easy to handle. 'Get out of here!'

'I see you have miraculously rediscovered your tongue.' Supremely at ease, Alex sank down on a corner of the bath, an unhidden smile of amusement curving his expressive mouth. Densely lashed golden eyes engaged on a boldly unapologetic survey of every gleaming wet inch of pale flesh on view. 'What a promising start to the new day...'

'I want you to listen to me.'

'I am a captive audience,' Alex assured her cheerfully.

Sara quivered with rage. If there was one thing she couldn't bear, it was *not* to be taken seriously. 'You're trying to behave as if yesterday never happened!'

A lean brown hand snaked out and caught her left hand, one long forefinger suggestively brushing the circle of bridal gold she wore. 'Didn't it?'

Deprived of one hand's anchorage, the towel dipped down dangerously low over her breasts and with a strangled hiss of mingled temper and mortification Sara dropped down into the water again. 'Go away!' she roared at him furiously.

'You're changing... You're changing into the woman you've always kept hidden and stifled,' Alex murmured with quiet satisfaction. 'The woman you were born to be. Fiery and passionate, not quiet and submissive. I saw it in Marco's studio first—all that you would conceal and all that I would set free.'

Sara opened her sultry mouth and closed it again, trembling with thwarted fury. 'Don't try to change the subject,' she finally shot back at him.

'Why would I do that? You needed to know the truth. I made no attempt to conceal it,' Alex reminded her. 'The brandy bottle was the one unknown, *cara*. I suspect that without that handicap you would have suspected the truth the same day. I did not foresee how rapidly events would move... or how swiftly our relationship would develop. I was prepared to *wait* for you to turn to me.'

'You don't even seem to appreciate the evil of what you've done!' Sara launched at him.

'The evil was Shorter's, *cara*. Don't make the mistake of laying the original sin at my door,' Alex warned her softly. 'Had he been faithful, I would have been powerless to interfere.'

'You had no *right* to interfere!'

'I saw my advantage and I used it. What else would you have expected me to do? If I hadn't intervened, you would have suffered a far more public betrayal. I don't believe that your fiancé had any intention of replacing you with your cousin... but the lady had other ideas,' Alex imparted with grim dark eyes. 'How much closer to the wedding would you have liked to come?'

Her teeth gritted. 'That's not relevant!'

'You think not? Without my "evil" intervention, *bella mia*, the invitations would have been out, the wedding presents arriving. Your cousin has a sense of the dramatic. I think she would have left it to the eleventh hour. You would have been greeted out of the blue by the announcement that they were in love. Would you have preferred that scenario?'

'Shut up, Alex!' Sara blitzed back at him rawly, wanting to cover her ears from his devious reasoning. *'Shut up!'*

Alex dealt her a uniquely cynical appraisal, his handsome mouth twisting. 'No, you would not have fallen over yourself for the opportunity to play the jilted bride, a sad object of pity to all concerned. You are far too proud to willingly subject yourself to such humiliation.'

'Damn you, Alex... I hate you!' Resentment was blazing out of control like a forest fire inside her.

'You married me to save face, *cara* ... If I have to live with that reality, why shouldn't you?' Alex drawled murderously quietly.

'You sneaky, manipulative swine!' Lunging forward without hesitation, Sara closed two angry hands over the hem of his immaculate grey jacket and tipped him backwards into the bath.

There was a burst of startled Italian, a resounding splash, a sudden dismaying weight on her extended lower limbs and then an instant of stark silence. And then Alex laughed. He threw back his handsome dark head and laughed with uninhibited appreciation.

'You asked for that,' Sara bit out mutinously, refusing to share in his amusement. 'Now perhaps you'll remove yourself.'

Alex bent forward and flipped off his shoes and socks. 'I don't think so,' he murmured, straightening his back lithely and shrugging his shoulders out of his jacket, pitching it carelessly aside.

'And what's that supposed to mean?'

He jerked his tie loose, then embarked on unbuttoning his shirt. 'I am where I want to be—'

'Let me up,' she instructed feverishly, pinned in place by the weight of his hard length.

Alex angled up his lean flanks to unzip his trousers and Sara took advantage of the movement to snake her legs back, but he was far too quick and agile for her. He flipped over and caught her arms before she could complete her escape and brought his mouth down hard on hers.

In a rage of incredulity, she meant to bite him, scratch him, pummel him with both furiously clenched fists. But at the same second that he fiercely probed her lips apart and delved between them with the stab of his tongue, she ran out of breath and reason and physical coordination. He devoured her with hot, hungry urgency and her hands briefly loosened and then clutched with helpless desperation as he yanked her up against him, crushing her bare breasts to the hard, muscular wall of his chest. She wanted more, so much more that every intoxicating second was only a frustrating preparation for the next. And then he released her.

In a daze she blinked as he sprang out of the bath, peeling off his shirt and dispensing with his sodden trousers and the clinging black briefs in a few impatient movements. He reached down into the water and swept her up as if she were an inanimate and dainty doll. Breathless confusion overwhelmed her. 'Put me down...put me down, Alex!'

'Getting me wet was a bad move, *cara*.' Brilliant golden eyes danced over her bemused face. '*Dio* ... it made the odds of you escaping unscathed from this bedroom about ninety-nine to one.'

'If you don't let go of...*me*!' Her wrathful response ended in a strangled yell as he dropped her down on the welcoming luxuriousness of the bed and she bounced.

Alex descended lithely onto the mattress, only to imprison her again, closing both hands over her wildly clawing ones and pressing them flat while at the same time lowering his lean, hard length to keep the rest of her in one place. 'Now...calm down—think,' he urged smoothly.

It struck her that about the very last thing she felt capable of just then was thinking. With every lethally sexy centimetre of Alex pinned to her damp, quivering flesh, rational thought was suspended by a sensation closer to pure panic than anything else. Already she could feel a sort of insidious heat and restive tension threatening her already shattered composure.

'Please—'

'I wanted you so much, *bella mia*...how could that ever be a crime?' Alex enquired, subjecting her to the full onslaught of eyes screened to a smouldering sliver of gold beneath inky black lashes. 'For a whole year I desired you and you held me at bay with cold, dismissive glances and scornful little smiles. You treated me like my father's wives once treated me—like an unavoidable but greatly to be regretted accident of birth. No man with red blood in his veins would have resisted the challenge.'

'Stop it,' Sara gasped, blocking him out by closing her eyes. She was trying so hard not to listen while at the same time endeavouring to stamp out the burgeoning and quite appalling sexual awareness leaping to life within her every skin cell, making her breath shorten, her heartbeat race and her pulses accelerate.

'You are my wife,' Alex reminded her very softly.

'I don't want to be!' Sara bit out shakily, tiny little quivers assailing her as she angrily fought to stamp out her own hatefully physical reaction to his proximity.

'This is very sudden,' Alex husked.

Temper took her again, strengthening her defiance. 'You think that if you chip away at me for long enough you can change the way I think...but you can't! Marco said I'd be safer with him that day and he was right. He told me to go for the two million and he was right about that too! You're just using me!' Sara condemned in sudden, bitter pain. 'And I'd rather be used for money than find myself trapped in a marriage that's a sleazy mockery of everything I believe in. At least the money would have been an *honest* exchange!'

Without warning, Alex freed her hands and sprang back from her. His strong dark features were harshly set. 'Is that what you really believe, *cara*?'

With a shaking hand, Sara fumbled for the sheet, wanting to cover herself all of a sudden from that look of icy derision in Alex's eyes. 'Yes,' she muttered chokily, knowing that she had told the truth of her feelings.

Of course he would never have offered and she would never have taken money, but the scenario she had forced herself to draw was far more apt in her opinion than the dubious respectability of the wedding ring she wore. A cruel, cheating charade was what Alex had really given her but she had entered their marriage with very different expectations, stupidly, naïvely trusting and believing in every assurance he had made. She recalled the manner in which he had smoothly tacked on the word 'eventually' to his supposed desire for children and she understood why now.

Alex had never planned on permanence. Alex had merely dangled a wedding ring as bait so that he could satisfy his lust and his ferocious need to win, whatever the cost. If she hadn't been so overly emotional, so eagerly willing to be swayed by his arguments, she would have suspected that reality far sooner. A male like Alex Rossini, with a father who changed wives the way other men changed their shirts, was highly unlikely to see the institution of marriage as an unbreakable bond. Alex had simply told her what she'd wanted and needed to hear.

Tears pricked her eyes again and filled her with a furious impatience at her own continuing and dismayingly unfamiliar emotionalism. She rolled herself under the sheet as if she were settling into her shroud.

Alex was already standing in the adjoining dressing room, rifling through drawers and cupboards, withdrawing fresh clothing. The significance of what he was doing slowly sank in on her as she abstractedly watched his every lithe, graceful movement. His sudden withdrawal had left her treacherous body aching, and her teeth clenched in shamed acknowledgement of the fact.

'This is your room?' she asked across the yawning gulf of silence, which she found quite unbearable.

'You were sleeping so soundly last night, I did not wish to disturb you.' His startlingly handsome features were shuttered, a cold contempt in his eyes which he made no attempt to conceal.

And for the first time Sara registered that Alex could affect her on a level that she had previously denied. A growing sense of fear and rejection was taking her over. Fear and rejection, she acknowledged dazedly. 'I will not hurt you', he had said, and yet he *was* hurting her. In fact all of a sudden her mind was toying with the cowardly notion that she had said too much, gone too far, offended too deeply... In dismay, she bit down so hard on her tongue to trap it between her teeth that she tasted blood. 'Submissive', he had called her. No, she was not going to be submissive or apologetic for honestly stating her own feelings. She had a right to say what she felt.

A right... a *right*—all too often suppressed and surrendered throughout her childhood. She had let herself be forced into a quiet, introverted little slot at an early age because if she'd dared to flex a finger out of that slot Antonia had been waiting, ready to break it. And she had been so grateful that her aunt and uncle had given her a home that she hadn't fought, hadn't defended herself, hadn't expressed herself in any way which might have caused offence or brought her into more open conflict with the daughter they adored. A little martyr of a peacemaker—that was what she had been and much good it had done her!

And where would she end up if one ferociously dirty look from Alex made her want to rush in and tactfully smooth things over as she had done with everyone all her life to date? She couldn't possibly be becoming emotionally attached to Alex. You hate him now, she reminded herself... but you *still* don't want him to leave this room. The discovery shattered her.

Alex emerged from the dressing room, immaculate again in a supremely sophisticated cream suit that was a spectacular foil for his golden skin and exotically dark eyes. And when did you start gaping at him all the time as if he were first prize in a lottery, eyeing him up like some sort of sex-obsessed teenager with uncontrollable hormones? she asked herself derisively.

In the midst of her increasingly frantic self-examination, Alex vented a soft, chilling laugh. Sara permitted her anxious gaze to wander guiltily back to him.

'You want to know why I married you?' he drawled. 'I thought you were different but I should have recalled that old adage that there's nothing new under the sun.'

'I thought you were different too.' But she wasn't going to share the fact that she had actually believed that he had miraculously been transformed from an arrogant, ruthless womaniser into a family man.

'You didn't care.' Alex shot her a glance from glittering dark eyes, his scorn palpable. 'Your cosy future was smashed and you wanted it back, whatever the cost or the risk. I had the means to give it to you—'

'I don't know what you're getting at.'

'Before my very eyes, I watched you fall in love with what I could buy you... and I shouldn't complain. I picked Ladymead out of two dozen properties as the one most likely to appeal. I played a winning bet. *Dio mio*...it did not occur to me that sometimes winning can feel more like losing.'

Sara had stilled, shaken by the information that he had taken her quite deliberately to Ladymead. That he could actually blame her for the results of his own relentlessly manipulative approach disconcerted her even more. 'You're not being fair—'

'I don't feel like being fair.' His wide mouth narrowed, clenched. 'For the first time I feel a certain sympathy for Shorter. I'm not surprised that he was tempted by a normal flesh-and-blood woman, who only wanted him and not some picture-book fantasy with a fairy castle and a perfect hero.'

'I didn't expect you to be perfect.' Her voice wobbled, betraying the strength of the blow he had dealt her. To hear herself compared unfavourably with Antonia pierced her on her weakest flank. 'But I did expect... honesty.'

'Only you don't like it when you get it. If I'd lied yesterday, you could have kept your rigid little principles intact and you would have generously shared your body with me last night,' he derided. 'But that wasn't the option I chose. I told you the truth without hesitation.'

'It's a matter of trust... can't you understand that?' Sara was horrified to realise that she was on the brink of tears again. 'I *trusted* you!'

'I don't think trust played that big a role in your decision to marry me,' Alex countered very drily, his expressive mouth twisting.

'Of course it did!'

'No, Sara. Your objective was to marry well and save face. I do believe I'm the male equivalent of a trophy wife in so far as you actually take notice of my existence. So don't accuse me of using you, *cara*. As I see it, I'm the one who's allowed himself to be used.'

'No—' she began painfully, her cheeks blazing so hotly that she felt as if she was burning up.

'You took not the smallest interest in the preparations for our wedding. As it was the opening chapter on our future together, I was less than impressed by the level of your commitment. Indeed, had I not intervened, you might well have gone up the aisle in the same dress you had chosen for another man's benefit!'

'No...' Sara mumbled sickly, belatedly grasping how very much she had taken for granted.

'I called you every day and all you could talk about was medieval glass, oak panelling and the complexities of renovating listed buildings! But the ultimate insult has to have been the presence of your ex at our wedding,' Alex informed her with icy precision. 'You had the time and the opportunity to prevent that development, but you didn't. There is no pretence of love between us but I found the spectacle of you clinging like a limpet to another man in front of *my* family and friends deeply offensive.'

Her stomach was churning with nausea now. Seen through Alex's eyes, her behaviour both before and during the wedding reached heights of crass insensitivity that she had never dreamt she could be capable of. She lowered her head, swallowing hard. 'No pretence of love between us', she thought wretchedly. No safe, secure raft of liking and bonding to fall back on when there was a crisis.

'And if you ever tell me again that you love him I will throw you out,' Alex completed with absolute conviction. 'I have not the faintest desire for your love but I will not tolerate the use of that kind of smug self-indulgence as a weapon...most especially not when it relates to a weak, lying, cheating little jerk who couldn't keep his pants on even within the family circle!'

The door shut with a thud. That was some exit, Alex, she conceded dazedly. Nothing like going out with a big bang. Nothing like pulling the ground from beneath my feet and changing the whole tenor of my outlook within the space of five agonisingly mortifying minutes.

Everything he had thrown at her had hit home hard. Guilty of bowing out on the wedding arrangements, guilty of yapping on ceaselessly about Ladymead, guilty of not having the guts to tell her relatives that she refused to have Brian at their wedding. After all, Alex, not her family, had paid for it all. And Brian's presence had ruined the day, making Sara feel self-conscious, strained and guiltily on the defensive.

Yes, she had fallen in love with Ladymead, but that was surely not a crime? The real problem had been that when Alex had phoned her their relationship had felt unreal to her. The house had seemed a safe subject to concentrate on. In a sense, too, she had been showing off. See, I can take care of all these things very efficiently without bothering you. See, I can turn that house into a home so fast you'll be really impressed, was what she had been trying to tell him. Only Alex had been anything but impressed.

And why should he have been? Alex had married her for sexual gratification, not for her home-making abilities...hadn't he? Yet that demeaning assumption no longer seemed to fall so neatly into place. Had she been overreacting to what she had learnt yesterday, letting her imagination, her insecurity run away with her? After all, she might still be shattered by the lengths to which Alex had gone in his determination to get her, but those same extremes surely indicated a great deal more than a mere fleeting sexual interest...didn't they?

Hesitantly Sara breathed in, a sense of greater calm enfolding her. For goodness' sake, she had been reacting like a neurotic! Alex had cunningly contrived the very existence of their relationship but that did not mean that absolutely everything he had told her was a lie! Alex might desire her but she could not believe that he would have sacrificed his freedom on that basis alone. Had her sole attraction been physical, Alex would have concentrated his brilliant powers of negotiation on persuading her into having an affair instead.

And on one other count Alex had also been right: it was wrong of her to keep on throwing up Brian. Brian was married to Antonia now...and it was extraordinary, she conceded, how little emotion she could currently stir in response to that reality. No, she was no longer hopelessly in love with her former fiancé. How could you continue to love a man who had turned out to be a figment of your imagination?

Brian had lied, cheated and deceived her, then abandoned her to the heat of everyone's anger while protecting himself. But she understood now what it seemed that her cousin had understood all along. Brian had really wanted both of them—Sara to be the good little wife, home-maker and supportive partner, Antonia for excitement, glamour and passion. And she herself had not given him that passion, so how could she really blame him for seeking it elsewhere? A rueful smile tinged Sara's mouth as she began to get dressed.

It was Alex she had to worry about now. So she had made mistakes...but then Alex had to. He had been too impatient. He had pushed the wedding through far too fast, denying her the time she had needed to adjust to their relationship. Well, whether Alex liked it or not, her necessary breathing space had come before the wedding and he had not aided his own cause by seeing her only twice during that period. Somehow, at the end of a phone line Alex had felt more like her boss again. She laughed at the idea, helplessly recalling Alex tipping backwards into the bath.

She was walking towards the grand staircase when a smiling young maid caught up with her. The girl extended a silver tray bearing an envelope with only one word slashed where the address should have been. Sara smiled too, seeing her own name inscribed in Alex's handwriting.

Alone again, she flipped open the envelope, her eyes sparkling with curiosity.

It was a cheque made out in her name for the sum of two million pounds.

CHAPTER SEVEN

HER cheeks as pink as wild roses, her heartbeat thundering at the foot of her throat, Sara crossed the floor of the echoing salon. The sheer grandeur of the vast reception room overpowered her.

'I thought we would dine out this evening,' Alex drawled. 'Would you like a drink before we leave?'

Sara shook her head in a quick, nervous motion, glossy streamers of ebony hair falling forward as she stole a glance down at the little black dress which had seemed the last word in sophistication when she'd bought it a week earlier. Now, set against the splendour of her surroundings, with Alex in a superb white dinner jacket, she had the suspicion that if she added an apron she would be easily mistaken for a waitress. She hovered, waiting for him to say something about the cheque, which she had immediately returned by the same method he had employed to deliver it.

Alex drained his crystal glass and set it down. 'Shall we go, then?'

Her teeth gritted. Was it for this response that she had spent an entire afternoon agonising upstairs? She had been so angry that she hadn't trusted herself to go near him, had deemed it wiser to take stock and cool down. 'That cheque...' she began stiltedly.

'I've opened an account for you instead. An honest exchange, you said.' Alex sent her a cool dark glance. 'Now that we understand each other I see no need for the commercial element to be discussed again.'

Sara drew in a deep breath, her heart lurching behind her breastbone. 'Alex...do you want a divorce?'

In the act of moving towards the door, Alex stopped dead and swung abruptly back to her.

'Because if that is what all this is about, why don't you just say so?' Sara continued, green eyes flashing like jewels against her pallor. 'I mean, let's not beat around the bush here, Alex. I have already received the message that I am a big disappointment and that nothing I have done over the last month has met with your approval—'

'I don't want a divorce.' His strong face was clenched hard, his dark gaze diamond-bright.

'Well, right now I just want to swim back to the airport,' Sara confided with an uneven little laugh, her stomach churning with nausea. 'I see "MISTAKE" looming in letters ten feet tall over that ceremony yesterday. I'm so very sorry for falling for the house you dangled like bait for my benefit . . . but I did not agree to marry you because you were rich! And until you wrote that cheque it didn't seriously occur to me that you could even think I could be that greedy. But if this is what you call marrying well I'm afraid you can blasted well keep it, Alex!'

As her voice fractured, betraying her distress, she spun away and began walking fast towards the door. But Alex moved faster, tugging her back to him with lean, determined hands. Closing his arms round her from behind, he expelled his breath in a pent-up hiss. 'I owe you an apology,' he grated roughly.

Sara was rigid. She squeezed her stinging eyes shut and trembled. So much pain—more pain than she had ever experienced, and that in itself was frightening. How did she say to him that she *did* have feelings for him but that she didn't know where they had begun or indeed even what they were but that the concept of losing him filled her with panic? And she couldn't even say that she liked him because, right now, she didn't like Alex at all. The cruelty of that cheque when he must surely have known that she was talking nonsense in her distress earlier—well, that kind of cruelty was utterly foreign to

Sara's nature. It scared her to feel in any way dependent on a male who could behave like that.

'It was my pride,' Alex confessed in a savage undertone as he bent his head down over hers. 'No woman has ever treated me with such indifference.'

'It wasn't indifference. You weren't there. It was all like a dream...coming up to the wedding,' she explained jerkily. 'We didn't feel real but the house *did*. And you were so distant on the phone...I felt awkward. I didn't know what you expected from me—'

'Too much.'

Her soft mouth wobbled and then compressed. 'I wanted you to be there. Too bad if you don't want to hear that—'

'*Dio*...it's exactly what I want to hear.'

'Is it?' she gulped.

'Even workaholics like to be missed now and again.' An uncertain shiver of amusement rippled through Sara as Alex spun her round to face him again.

He gazed down at her, and a long forefinger followed the silvery path of a tear stain on her cheek before taking a detour to the tremulous softness of her lower lip. There he lingered to trace that sensitive fullness. Her breath got snarled up in her throat, her slender body tautening in involuntary response to the sizzling sexual energy emanating from him. 'If I'd known, I'd have flown you out,' he remarked reflectively. 'You wouldn't have seen much of me by day but at least we would have had the nights.'

Maybe all men had a one-track mind, Sara found herself thinking, with a regret that was not for sharing. It would have been more of a compliment if Alex had contrived to think of something other than the sexual benefits of her company. But then perhaps she was also guilty of expecting too much too soon. A marriage of convenience had to start somewhere, she reminded herself squarely.

'I wasn't *using* you,' Sara whispered feverishly, struggling to put her thoughts in order but finding it impossible. All she could really feel was enormous relief that the cold gulf that he had imposed between them had been bridged. 'You were there and I . . . needed you.'

His dark face tautened. 'And I need you now, *cara*.' Alex delivered the words with another meaning entirely as he dropped one hand down to the swell of her hips and arranged her into more intimate contact with his powerful thighs. A clenching sensation low in the pit of her stomach made her jerk as she felt the hard thrust of his manhood. Her knees suddenly had all the consistency of jelly and her hands flew up to grip his shoulders. 'A month is a very long time for me.'

And dinner was now a long way off, she sensed, her cheeks burning fierily. With a husky laugh of satisfaction, Alex raked shimmering golden eyes of desire over her and suddenly swept her off her feet and up into his arms. 'You still blush like a virgin,' he teased, starting towards the door.

She felt hot all over when he put her down again in the bedroom and slid down the zip on her dress. This is all right, she told herself urgently; this is normal, natural, healthy behaviour. We're married. It's OK to want him so much that you're ashamed of yourself. It is not OK to start imagining you're just a sex object again. Narrow-minded prudes are boring.

The dress pooled round her feet. She resisted an instinctive urge to cover herself. Alex's gaze locked with hers. His sensual mouth slashed into a knowing smile.

She broke breathlessly into speech. 'Alex, I—'

But, reaching for her, he bent his dark, well-shaped head and silenced her with the heat of his hungry mouth. And the ground shifted below her feet. He kissed her and there was nothing but him and the hot, swirling darkness behind her lowered eyelids. She stood on tiptoe and kissed him back with all the helpless urgency of her own need, her heartbeat a wild thunder in her ears, the blood in her veins pulsing at supersonic speed. She was dizzy when he lifted his head again, her passion-glazed eyes clinging to his.

He undid the catch on her lacy white bra and she stopped breathing altogether as he curved a hand round the pointed swell of one bared breast and brushed his thumb across its pouting pink nipple. A whimper of sound escaped low in her throat as an electric jolt of pleasure shot through her, the distended peaks of her breasts achingly sensitive to his awakening touch. He backed her down onto the bed, stood over her while he undressed. Smouldering golden eyes raked over her and he smiled with satisfaction.

'You *always* wanted me,' he said.

Her mind locked back into gear. 'No...'

But the accusation lingered and sent her memory flying back through countless uneasy encounters when she had dipped her eyes, turned her head and closed her mind even to an admission of what she was doing. She had blocked Alex out over and over again—so often that it had become a habit never, ever to relax around him, always to feel strained, threatened...

'You had iron self-discipline...and you were stubborn. You knew the attraction was there between us but you wouldn't admit it. It drove me crazy,' Alex told her, peeling off his shirt without once removing his intent gaze from her bemused face. 'I was afraid to make a move in case you walked out. You kept a wall between us, you never came close...you never touched me, not even accidentally.'

Involuntarily she recalled innumerable instances of her own pronounced caution in his radius. Remembering scared her. It was scary to accept that all along her body had been conscious of this powerful attraction but that her mind had resisted even acknowledging it until that day when he had walked into her office and she had told herself that she was *not* susceptible. That had been her first conscious admission of what Alex could make her feel. 'I didn't know,' she muttered

'You do now.' Alex folded himself lithely down on the bed beside her and tugged her into his arms, and the thinking stopped there as if he had pushed a button. Her nostrils flared with the scent of him and she trembled as his long, lean muscularity connected with her. She met his eyes and burned in the defenceless heat of anticipation, her breasts rising and falling with the quickening of her breathing, excitement stirring so fast again that it took her by storm.

He lowered his head and let the tip of his tongue graze a rose-pink bud, skimming a hand up over the tautness of her quivering ribcage, discovering the thunder of her racing heartbeat as her whole body leapt in response to that tiny caress.

'Alex...' she gasped.

'Feeling like this is special, *bella mia*,' he muttered raggedly. '*Dio*...you are so beautiful.'

With unsteady fingers she caressed his cheekbone, wanting, wanting him so much that it was like a pain inside her as her thighs tightened on the ache in her loins. His eyes narrowed with smoky desire and then he curved his hands round her pale breasts, touching, inciting her pouting nipples before he dropped his mouth there and tugged at the tormented peaks with an erotic precision that engulfed her in a scorching surge of sensation. Her fingernails dug into the hard muscles of his back and then pushed through his hair as her body rose up to his of its own volition, tiny little gasps of sensual pleasure tearing free from deep in her throat.

His fingers stroked the smooth skin of her inner thigh, mounting higher by torturous degrees that made her clutch at him in involuntary protest, drag him up again, find his mouth again for herself and exult in the hungry thrust of his tongue. He skimmed a finger over the satin mound of her bikini pants so that she twisted and moaned under his mouth in a sweet agony of desperate need. And then the frustrating barrier was gone and he was expertly exploring the honeyed dampness beneath, sending her swerving violently out of control, every muscle screaming with tension as her heartbeat hammered.

'*Now*...' Alex groaned when she was on the brink of an intolerable excitement.

Her gaze collided blindly with his and then he pulled her up to receive him and drove into her hard and fast and her head fell back and she cried out with the hot, torturous pleasure of that penetration, her body yielding to the forceful possession of his. He moved again with sinuous eroticism and the pleasure increased to such unbearable limits that she lost herself entirely. With every tormenting stroke he took her higher and her nails raked down his smooth back as her spine arched and the sunburst heat in her loins suddenly expanded, every muscle clenching in response as she went flying over the edge into a release that convulsed her in violent waves.

In the aftermath she clung to him, recalling the wondrously intimate feel of him shuddering with that same satisfaction in the circle of her arms. A glorious sense of well-being enclosed her. She was at peace, perfectly at peace, until she became aware of the intense happiness which was fostering that quiet contentment. It was that unquestionable feeling of joy which shook Sara the most.

Alex rolled over, carrying her with him, and her arms instinctively tightened round his hot, damp, sleekly muscled length because... because she didn't want to let him go. Concealed by the wild tumble of her hair as she rested her cheek against his shoulder, her eyes flew wide at that alarming awareness. She also recognised within herself a surge of raw feminine possessiveness and that made her shiver in shock.

'Cold?' Alex tugged the sheet up carefully over her and shifted again beneath her, like a cat stretching in sunlight. She knew that he was smiling. 'Much better without the brandy,' he murmured huskily.

Sara tensed. 'I wasn't drunk.'

'But you weren't *quite* sober either,' Alex interposed with rueful emphasis. 'I promised you that you could trust me that night. I wasn't lying when I said that, *bella mia*. But I overestimated the limits of my self-control. I didn't really care why you wanted me. It was enough that you did.'

One crazy night, Sara thought, and it had changed her life. 'Why all the flowers?' she whispered curiously.

'Guilt,' he said succinctly.

'Guilt?' She pushed her hair out of her eyes and looked up at him with a frown.

His expressive mouth twisted. 'I wasn't expecting it to be your first time, *cara*. For a woman that is a significant event and you weren't a teenager any more, you were twenty-three, which suggested that abstention had been a deliberate policy. I didn't think you were likely to feel as reckless in the morning as you had the night before.'

'You were right.' Her creamy skin turned pink and if she hadn't still been too shy to discuss their intimacy of that night she might have told him that he had made it a very significant event. Even in her angry turmoil of regret, she had known that Alex had made their love-making feel special. But then why not? she reflected ruefully. Alex was a very experienced lover. At a tender nineteen, an age when *she* had still been at the stage of fumbling kisses on doorsteps, Alex had been living in no doubt very exciting sin with an older woman. Who had seduced whom? she wondered, and then suppressed the thought, scolding herself for such tasteless, inappropriate curiosity.

Alex absorbed the distant look in her green eyes. His dark scrutiny glittering, he lifted her away from him and tumbled her carelessly down onto a cool patch in the spacious bed as he slid out of it. 'I'm hungry, *cara*. There's still plenty of time to make dinner.'

His abrupt withdrawal sharply disconcerted Sara. She watched him stroll into the bathroom, stared in consternation at the scratches marring the smooth, bronzed perfection of his back and dropped her head again, the warmth of that curious joy inside her ebbing fast. She began to wonder fearfully if the only time she would feel secure and important to Alex was when he was in bed with her, satisfying his desire.

But why should she need more security? Hadn't she agreed to what Alex had termed 'a practical marriage'? She couldn't expect to move the goalposts now, mustn't start to look for the kind of affectionate extras that only came naturally with love. This was a male who gave flowers out of guilt. The beribboned baskets had not been the attempted romantic gesture that she had dimly and foolishly imagined them to be. Romance was out of the question too. Sex was in, sentiment was out.

He had been very honest about that. Alex valued that quality of emotional detachment in a relationship. And very possibly that was why he had married a woman in love with another man. Had it ever crossed his mind that that same woman might have fallen right back out of love again without even knowing it? Had it ever occurred to him that a woman who had been hurt and humiliated and then pursued by a fantastically handsome, sexy and strong male might find the image of her disappointing first love wholly obscured by his own?

For that, Sara registered dazedly, was what had happened. Brian's presence at their wedding had filled her with only a great deal of self-conscious embarrassment. She had felt no bitterness, no jealousy of Antonia and no regret. It had been Alex who'd consumed her thoughts. It had been Alex who'd taught her the meaning of desire, Alex who'd overshadowed Brian to such an extent that within the space of a day her former fiancé had inspired her with nothing but a need to run the other way.

But no, she wasn't foolish enough to start imagining that she was falling in love with Alex now. She was bound to feel *some* sort of attachment to him, she reasoned fiercely. After all, they were married; they were lovers. She understood perfectly what was happening inside her mind. A kind of natural bonding to Alex was taking place...only there had been nothing remotely bonding about the manner in which he had literally dumped her off him just now!

Her teeth clenched as she thrust her wildly tousled hair out of her flashing eyes. Her trophy husband indeed! Her perfect hero! He satisfied one appetite and immediately thought of the next. No, he needn't worry too much about inciting her to feelings of forbidden love and devotion!

'First love?'

Sara's nose wrinkled. 'You'll laugh...'

'I won't.'

'OK...I was fifteen. It was a crush, all that moony love-from-afar stuff,' Sara muttered dismissively. 'I saw him every day for weeks when I was walking home from school. He was part of the road gang who built the bypass. You said you *wouldn't* laugh!' In hot-cheeked reproach, Sara threw a grape at Alex, which he caught one-handed and crushed slowly between even white teeth while he endeavoured to silence his mirth. 'He was very fanciable when he took his shirt off.'

Alex tilted his tousled dark head back, a vibrant smile curing his sensual mouth. 'Beefcake appeal, *bella mia*? I'm surprised at you.'

'Are you really?' Widening dancing green eyes, Sara treated him to a slow, sweeping survey that started at his broad, bronzed shoulders, slid down over his magnificent torso to his narrow waist and finally ended at the muscular, darkly haired thigh half-exposed by the tangled bedsheets.

'Funny, I would say that in that department I haven't changed one bit.'

Alex reached out, knotted a punitive lean hand into her torrent of hair and drew her down to him. 'Vixen,' he reproved her softly, brushing his mouth provocatively across the swollen fullness of hers, and her heart skipped an entire beat, a familiar tide of immediate hunger washing over her, leaving her weak.

It didn't matter how often Alex made love to her. She had found that out over the past two weeks. Alex could awaken that wanting at will. She had stopped trying to fight it. The blood sang in her veins with a wanton anticipation that could still make her blush. As she curved into the hard heat of him, she felt the thrusting readiness of his arousal against her and the ache between her thighs intensified shamelessly. He kissed her breathless, then pinned her willing body under him with an earthy groan of satisfaction and sent her out of her mind with pleasure all over again.

'It's getting late!' Alex sprang out of bed, ruthlessly hauled the sheet from her warm, drowsy flesh. 'We're going out,' he reminded her mockingly.

Minutes later she stood under the shower trying to wake up again, envying Alex his electrifying energy. She looked dazedly back on days which had flown by in a whirl of constant activity. Alex seemed to need to busily fill every waking moment they shared. But why had she ever worried that she had made a mistake when she'd married him? she asked herself now.

Alex had the power to make her feel incredibly special. Alex had plunged her into a luxurious life of complete indulgence, and nobody had ever indulged Sara's wants and wishes before. Being spoilt, she had discovered, took a lot of getting used to but it had certainly done wonders for her shaky self-esteem. She had reeled dizzily through day after wonderful day of Alex's exclusive attention.

First he had taken her shopping. Now she had a wardrobe stuffed with gorgeous designer clothes, most of them outfits that she wouldn't have dared even to look at had not Alex insisted, and for the first time Sara found herself taking a real pride in her appearance. 'Such a shame that Sara's so plain,' she had heard her grandmother complain once after fondly admiring her other grandchild's blue-eyed blonde prettiness. Sara had never felt beautiful in her life until Alex had said that she was, and, secure in the conviction that in *his* eyes she was not unattractive, she was beginning to see herself in a very different light.

He took so much interest in her, in every tiny thing about her. He had had to dig through all the layers of her conviction that she was a deeply boring person to get her to open out without apology or embarrassment. But he had persisted and he had listened. Was he always like this with her sex—a stunningly charismatic male who was highly attuned to the female psyche, who knew exactly what it took to make a woman feel not only desirable but also fascinating? Or was this current intensity more typical of Alex at the start of a new affair... before the boredom set in? She hurriedly squashed that pessimistic thought flat.

'Wear the gold dress,' Alex suggested.

'Won't it be a bit... flashy?'

'I like flashy on you. And you owe me,' Alex drawled teasingly.

'For what?'

'For destroying my appreciation of beauty with a year of ugly navy and brown suits.'

She laughed, caught the reflection of her own smile in a mirror as she dressed. There were stars in her eyes, and she had a crazy, irrepressible feeling of happiness that was becoming more and more familiar with every day that passed. Quickly she looked away again. But there was no avoiding what was going on inside her heart. Her head had nothing at all to do with it. Intelligence couldn't stop her pulses jumping every time Alex came within ten feet of her.

And if she was falling head over heels in love with her own husband it was not *her* fault, it was his. When a man made a woman feel this wonderful, what did he expect to earn in response? Cold, polite detachment? No doubt Alex wanted to make up for the rocky start of their marriage but, even so, he really did seem to care about her. He had to have cared to have asked her to marry him so quickly. He had to have wanted her an awful lot. It disconcerted Sara to realise that the manipulation that she had been so shocked by on their wedding day had now become something she hugged to herself as proof of the depth of Alex's desire for her.

'You look incredibly sexy...'

She turned. Cut on the bias, the fluid, simple lines of the gold shoestring-strapped dress accentuated the slender perfection of her figure. The gorgeous fabric shimmered seductively with her every movement.

'But rather bare...' Alex turned her back to the mirror and brushed her hair out of his path. He slid a slender diamond necklace round her throat, his cool, deft fingers brushing the nape of her neck as he fastened it. 'I bought earrings as well,' he murmured huskily. 'But they won't do. Your ears aren't pierced. *Not* very observant of me.'

Her fingertips shyly brushed the glittering jewels and her eyes suddenly stung. 'It's gorgeous, Alex ... Thank you.'

'It's been an incredible two weeks, *bella mia*. I believe the pleasure has all been mine.' Alex let his lips feather briefly, caressingly across one bare shoulder and then he drew lithely back and enveloped her in a soft velvet evening jacket.

Grasping his hand, Sara stepped uncertainly onto the motor-launch, not quite accustomed as yet to the wholly frivolous height of her strappy sandals. They dined out almost every evening but the enchantment of Venice by night could not fade. The splendid façades of the *palazzo* along the Grand Canal were floodlit, and against the rich indigo backdrop of the night sky and the dark, reflective water the sight was a magical one.

As the launch moved off, illuminated by the dazzling lights that framed the Rialto Bridge, Sara watched Alex with compulsive intensity. Sometimes she wanted so badly to get inside that sleek dark head and root around for answers that made sense. *Why me?* she wanted to ask suddenly. What was so special about me? She was an ordinary girl from an ordinary background and Alex was an immensely wealthy male with a blue-blooded pedigree that could be traced back centuries. He could have married any woman, yet he had chosen to marry her.

Was it utter madness or shocking vanity for her to wonder if Alex could be just a *little* in love with her? Maybe it was the shock of being treated with such incredible consideration and generosity which was encouraging her to cherish so wild a hope. No womaniser ever got successful by being less than charming, she reminded herself doggedly. He knows women inside out. Turning your head is probably just an ego-trip for him. Six months from now maybe he'll be treating you like a piece of furniture, any thrill you ever had for him staled by familiarity...so enjoy the Rolls-Royce treatment while it lasts.

'What's the matter with you?' Alex enquired as he handed her out of the launch onto solid ground again.

Sara tensed. 'Nothing.'

'You're very quiet.' Alex slanted a grim dark scrutiny over her taut profile. 'I suppose it was too much to hope that you would forget...'

'Forget what?' Sara queried, dismayed by the speed with which Alex's mood could change.

'Don't play games, *cara*. This is, after all, the day when you expected to drift blissfully up the aisle into Shorter's waiting arms!'

Sara was shocked by the unwelcome reminder. She turned pale, thinking that Alex only had to mention Brian and it was like having a freezer door slammed in her face. It was little wonder that she went out of her way to ensure that she never accidentally referred to the man who had been a big part of her life for almost two years.

'No, I did not think you were unaware of the fact,' Alex said very drily. 'You've put on quite an act today but it's beginning to wear thin.'

'Is it?' Sara gazed up at him, anxious green eyes clinging to the starkly handsome lines of his dark features, a distinctly strained smile curving her tense mouth. 'Alex, I'd actually forgotten that this was the day.'

His brilliant eyes hardened. He said something in Italian—something derisively suggestive of disbelief.

'I *had*!'

'I know that certain look on your face.' Alex thrust open the door of the exclusive restaurant.

'No, you don't,' Sara protested, suddenly angry at being unfairly accused.

The conversation came to a frustrating halt as the *maître d'* surged forward with alacrity. He was showing them to their table when a silver-haired older man thrust his chair noisily back nearby and rose with an exclamation. 'Alex?' The rest was in volatile Italian.

'Sara...' Alex drew her smoothly forward. 'Tony Bargani, a family friend.'

'You must join us.' Tony snapped his fingers imperiously to call up more chairs and settled her down firmly in his own seat. 'Alex knows everyone. My wife, Claudia.' He patted the shoulder of the stunning silver-blonde beside Sara with distinct pride of possession. 'Guy Chilton and his wife, Denise...'

Guy Chilton was already up, enthusiastically shaking hands. Tony was calling for drinks. His wife, who must have been a good twenty years his junior, was too busy competing for Alex's attention to take account of Sara.

The American woman, Denise, sighed with a wry smile. 'I believe this is your honeymoon, Sara. You should have avoided us. The men will be talking business for the rest of the evening.'

Claudia dropped down into her seat again and sent Sara a flickering glance of amusement. 'I'm quite sure Sara knows the score, Denise. She used to work for Alex, and with Alex business always come first and last. I remember my time with him well.'

'You used to work for Alex?' Sara smiled.

Claudia widened her eyes and uttered a sharp little laugh. 'Darling, do I really look as though I ever worked nine to five in some menial little office job? How frightfully uncomplimentary!'

Faint colour stained Sara's cheeks as the upper-class English accent cut through her. 'I'm sorry. I misunderstood.'

'Hardly surprising.' Claudia turned hostile blue eyes on her. 'I expect you're feeling rather out of your depth in this milieu.'

With difficulty, Sara kept her apologetic smile in place. 'I'm learning all the time.'

Tony toasted them with champagne, his natural warmth in strong contrast to his wife's air of dismissive boredom. 'I'm surprised the two of you aren't on the yacht,' he commented.

'Sara gets seasick,' Alex returned casually.

Her dark head shot up, surprise etched in her eyes. 'Who told you that?'

'Your aunt.' Across the table, rich dark eyes locked with hers, amusement shimmering in their depths. 'At the reception. The news necessitated a decidedly last-minute change of destination—'

'You mean you didn't know?' Tony's portly frame shook with mirth.

Sara hadn't known either. And if she could have got hold of her aunt at that instant she would have strangled her! One sickly day trip to France while she had still been at school was scarcely sufficient evidence on which to base such an assumption.

'How very inconvenient.' Claudia oozed sympathy. 'Will you be selling *Sea Spring* now?'

'Certainly not for my benefit. My aunt tends to exaggerate,' Sara interposed ruefully.

'Venice has to be the most romantic city in the world,' Denise Chilton commented warmly. 'I can't think of anywhere more wonderful to spend your honeymoon.'

'But then you didn't grow up here...Alex did,' Tony's wife slotted in sweetly.

A near-overpowering desire to empty her glass over Claudia's head assailed Sara as the first course was delivered.

The meal progressed. Alex smoothly engaged Tony in conversation. Sara's cheeks stopped burning. Their hostess was one of Alex's exes, Sara gathered grimly, dumped with the roses and the diamonds and still simmering over the blow to her ego. She would have to develop a thicker skin for such encounters.

'You know, the resemblance *is* really quite remarkable,' Claudia murmured very quietly over the coffee-cups when Denise had disappeared off to the cloakroom.

Sara lifted her head. 'Sorry?'

'Alex's father and Tony are old friends. We dined with them in London last week. Apparently Sandro was staggered the first time he saw you,' Claudia continued very softly.

'I'm afraid I don't follow...'

'You're the living image of Alex's one and only true love.' Claudia's eyes were bright with spiteful amusement. 'Sandro got a shock when he saw you coming down the aisle. For a moment he thought you *were* Elissa. Silly, of course...she'd be twenty years older than you now...but don't they say that everyone has a double somewhere?'

A creeping veil of coldness was slowly enclosing Sara. Her brain was in a fog. She could not seem to absorb what Claudia was telling her.

'I never actually met her,' Claudia confided. 'But when Tony and I got home I dug out some old family photo albums to satisfy my curiosity.'

'Family albums?' Sara questioned with a frown.

'Elissa was married to Tony's cousin at the time she took off with Alex...didn't you know that?'

Sara's tongue snaked out to moisten her dry lower lip. 'His cousin?' she said weakly, shooting an involuntary glance at the three men on the other side of the table, who were enjoying an animated, friendly conversation. Elissa had been married when Alex met her?

'You do have a lot to learn. Everyone blamed *her*, even Tony. Alex was only a boy and she was one devastating lady. Very petite, hourglass figure, long black hair just like you. Alex never did get over her. She turned him into a cold bastard. But then you're something special, aren't you?' Claudia touched her glass against the rim of Sara's in a mocking toast. 'Only with you can Alex relive his fantasy...and he doesn't even need to switch off the light!'

CHAPTER EIGHT

'I FEEL like a bath...' Sara mumbled, heading for the *en suite* bathroom like a homing pigeon seeking sanctuary.

'Sara, did Claudia say something to upset you?'

Sara paused, her slim back rigid, and then turned her dark head. 'What on earth could she have said?' she managed with apparent blankness.

Alex loosened his tie and surveyed her with intent dark eyes that were sharp enough to strip paint. 'Five years ago I met her at a wedding and invited her to a dinner party. She amused herself by shredding the looks and reputation of every other woman present. She's poisonous. I didn't see her again, nor did I sleep with her.'

Hot colour had drenched Sara's former pallor. 'You don't need to explain that to me,' she told him uncomfortably.

'Because you really don't care either way, do you, *cara*?' A tiny muscle pulled taut at the corner of Alex's compressed mouth, his narrowed eyes more slivers of glittering gold intensity as he stared back at her.

'It's not like that...I mean, I'm not an idiot,' she muttered, her head pounding with so much tension that she was beginning to feel physically sick. 'I know you have a past...obviously.'

'And a wife who doesn't have a jealous, possessive bone in her body. I am so fortunate,' Alex breathed with the suggestion of gritted teeth.

Sara looked back at him, bewildered by a dialogue which barely a tenth of her brain could concentrate on. 'Alex...I'm not feeling very well,' she whispered strickenly, her stomach twisting more than ever with the tension in the room.

'You don't need to make excuses and you don't need to hide in the bathroom either,' Alex delivered in a slashing undertone. 'I have no desire to share the same bed with you tonight!'

Bewilderment seized Sara as he strode out of the room. Her wretched tummy heaved. She fled into the bathroom and was very much preoccupied for some minutes. Finally, she rested her perspiring forehead against the cold surround of the bath and slowly got a grip on herself again before she began to undress. Claudia Bargani was vindictive. Alex had said it, Sara *knew* it for a fact. Normally she wouldn't have given credence to anything such a woman told her. But Claudia's revelation had still plunged Sara into deep shock. Why? Because taken in tandem with Sara's sudden marriage that revelation threatened to make a terrifying kind of sense.

Could Alex have wanted her only because she reminded him of Elissa? Did Alex even realise what might have attracted him to her? Or could the similarity be so striking that he had immediately recognised it? Whichever, she was left with the degrading possibility that she might well owe her present position as Alex's wife to something as agonisingly superficial as her face and her body. Not to mention being left at the mercy of a lot of really creepy, utterly degrading thoughts, she reflected in a tempest of angry pain.

Everyone had been stunned when Alex had married her. Sara had been stunned too when he'd proposed. She had been equally shaken by the discovery that Alex had been wildly attracted to her for the entire year that she had worked for him. But if she reminded Alex of the woman he had loved and lost, the woman he had never forgotten, what made her worthy of such obsessive desirability now seemed obvious. Was it possible that she owed everything they had shared since their marriage to the memory of another woman? The intensity of his interest, the exclusive attention, the extra-ordinary passion...?

She knew that she was tearing herself apart—in short, doing exactly what Claudia had wanted her to do—but she couldn't seem to stop doing it. But maybe Claudia had simply made it all up; maybe Claudia had a wildly inventive imagination. Sara curled up in a tight ball in a bed that felt horribly big, cold and empty. She was so tense that her muscles hurt, but it didn't really matter because it seemed to her that every fibre of her being was in agony.

She loved Alex...but suddenly she hated him too—for having the power to put her through such mental hoops of fire. Wild images of revenge swept her imagination. In every one of them Alex stood looking totally defeated while she packed her bags with frigid dignity and disdain and left him flat, publicly deserted him after two weeks of marriage. The door opened. She sat up with a jerk, switched on the bedside lights.

Alex was already standing beside the bed, quite magnificently nude and characteristically unconcerned by the fact.

'What do you want?' she demanded fierily.

'You,' Alex said succinctly.

Anger gleamed like a hurricane warning in his golden gaze and her engrossing revenge scenario sagged like a sofa bereft of its stuffing. Alex was a long way from total defeat. Aggression emanated from every line of his lithe, sun-bronzed body as he slid into bed and reached for her with hands far too strong to be easily evaded. In one smooth movement he forced her down and flat again, anchoring her furious body into stillness with his own.

Her teeth clenched in disbelief. 'If you don't get off me, Alex, I'll hit you!'

Alex propped his chin on the heel of one hand, his tawny eyes ablaze with very male provocation. 'Be my guest,' he challenged.

Her hands bunched into fists. He lowered his glossy dark head and took her mouth with a raw heat that scorched. A splintering shard of answering passion pierced her, overpowering every other sense. He bruised her lips and yet still her hands opened out and clutched at him with a hunger she couldn't deny. Indeed the hunger felt sharper, stronger, more desperate than ever before, leaving her utterly defenceless. He leant back from her when she was breathless, her heartbeat racing fast enough to choke her, every skin cell and pulse thrumming with wild response.

As she struggled to focus on his intent dark profile, he closed hard fingers over the fragile silk screening her heaving breasts and quite coolly ripped it away, the sound of the rending fabric preternaturally loud in the throbbing silence. Momentarily Sara went stiff with fright, and then she watched his hand curve round the pouting swell of her own naked flesh, his thumb grazing across a straining pink nipple, and a hot, deep melting started inside her, reducing her to boneless, quivering collusion.

He let his tongue flick over the achingly sensitive peak and a strangled whimper escaped her as her whole body pushed up to him in an unstoppable wave of response. He lifted his head again, glittering gold eyes sweeping over her as he wrenched her free of the tangled remnants of silk confining her legs. He ran a sure hand back up the tightening length of one slender thigh and discovered the moist warmth of her most delicate flesh, and the spiralling excitement that he could evoke with the tiniest caress sent her ever more violently out of control.

'No, I didn't think you would hit me...' Alex murmured softly, chillingly.

She fought through the wanton layers of her own suffocating pleasure and struggled to think again. 'What...?' she mumbled, relocating her voice an equal challenge.

'I touch you and you wouldn't hear a fire alarm. I touch you at any time of the day or the night and it's instant surrender. You've taught me that in two short weeks. All the sex that I want, whenever I want.'

'A-Alex, what are you—?'

'Saying?' Smouldering golden eyes locked with hers with icy precision. '*Dio*...I am not complaining, *bella mia*. But what a waste of a year. I was needlessly cautious to a degree that now embarrasses me. Sexually harassing you between the filing cabinets would have been a hugely entertaining exercise... You can't keep your hands off me even in the middle of a fight! So if you have to languish over the pretty blond boy you lost, why should I be offended? Between the sheets you're still incredibly willing to satisfy my most basic needs...*and* your own.'

Eyes wide, Sara was rigid with shock until it belatedly dawned on her for the very first time that Alex might actually be jealous—a suspicion that made his verbal offensive wash over her. 'I wasn't thinking about Brian,' she said quietly, intently, wanting to convince him, and she would have said a great deal more with very little encouragement.

But she didn't get the encouragement. In coolly insolent response, Alex scanned the length of her naked body, so trustingly open to his gaze, before he met her anxious eyes again. 'Not right now, no,' he conceded with a pointed derision that was like a slap in the face. 'But, you see, I expect your full attention *out* of bed too. Feel free to agonise as much as you like over Shorter...but from now on I suggest you indulge your sentiments in private. Your tragedy-queen mood with its accompanying deathly silence sets my teeth on edge.'

And Sara shrank inside herself, the illusion that he might have been becoming jealous of that former love brutally, instantaneously dissolved. Her struggle to hide her growing distress earlier had meant only one thing to Alex once she had denied that Claudia had played any part in her change of mood. He had assumed that Brian was behind her withdrawal—a belief that had provoked not jealousy but coldly sardonic impatience and reproof. Love him all you like, was the message she'd received. Just don't bore me to death with your silly emotionalism.

And *that* was when Sara felt unbearably, hideously humiliated. She read the other message that Alex was giving her too: her undeniable ability to behave like a wanton slut in bed was just about the only thing he did appreciate about her! With a frantic hand she snatched at the sheet and dragged it clumsily over bared skin that now shamed her. She curved defensively away from him, her flesh clammy. Alex used her own body like a weapon against her. He made her feel cheap. 'Cold and detached,' Pete had said. She stared strickenly into those stunningly golden but frighteningly unreadable eyes and shivered compulsively, as if she were looking into the jaws of death, repulsed by her own vulnerability.

Alex frowned, muttered something fierce in Italian and tugged her firmly back against his warm, muscular length. In bitter pain, she felt the familiar surge of her own body against his and knew that he could make her want him no matter what he did, and that chilled and mortified her even more. She froze in instinctive rejection. 'Don't touch me.'

His strong muscles clenched hard. 'Sara...I'm finding out that I can't live with being the consolation prize. If you want to stay married to me, you have to put the love of your life behind you,' he spelt out with hard emphasis.

Reacting to the part of that threat which related to their marriage, Sara turned white. 'As you did with Elissa?' she whispered feverishly.

His ebony brows drew together. '*Madre di Dio* ...what—?'

'Because you can't say you put her behind you, can you?' Sara suddenly launched at him an entire octave higher.

'Elissa doesn't come into this!' Alex dismissed with raw, stinging impatience.

Sara turned her head away, her heart thumping at the foot of her throat. 'I heard someone say... at our wedding... that I looked like her...'

The words lay there between them. The pulsing silence seemed to stretch endlessly. She was holding her breath. 'Alex?' she finally prompted very, very tautly.

There was slight movement beside her and the lights went out.

'No comment,' Alex murmured without any expression at all.

The response stunned Sara. She lay there rigid in the darkness but Alex made no further move towards her. However, there was nothing tense about the drowsy sigh of positively indolent satisfaction that escaped him as he shifted against the fine linen sheets and then lay with the stillness of complete relaxation—a reality soon borne out by the deep, even sound of his breathing as he fell asleep... while Sara lay awake.

The honeymoon was over.

Alex dealt her a measuring look in the limousine carrying them across London. 'You look tired. You should go straight back to bed.'

'I'm fine. I have to unpack—'

'The staff will do the unpacking. You might as well rest. I'll be late tonight,' he told her.

Sara stiffened. 'Then I'll go down to Ladymead, see how the work is going.'

'I should check out the workforce first,' Alex murmured with lazy mockery, dark eyes flicking over her strained face. 'If a brawny plasterer takes off his shirt in your radius, I might be history before I know it.'

'Very funny, Alex.' Flames of colour burnished in her pallor.

'I never did tell you who my first love was—'

'You mean your memory goes back that far?'

Alex smiled, his mood infuriatingly buoyant. 'I was twelve. She was thirteen. I lied about my age. She blushed every time she looked at me. She had skin like a peach, black curly hair and braces on her teeth. For the whole of one week I was enraptured.'

'The longevity of your affections is remarkable.'

Alex laughed appreciatively, his dark, flashing eyes colliding with hers. 'When she found out I was younger, she cut me dead!'

An involuntary smile crept across the tense line of her mouth, a giant wave of love surging up inside her. She veiled her shadowed eyes immediately but she was angry with herself now for lying awake all night brooding. Alex had never promised to love her, had he? He had said that he could make her happy and he had, but he had also shattered her illusion that she could somehow have more. Maybe she had needed that lesson. It had been very foolish of her to imagine that simply because she had fallen in love Alex might have too.

So she *did* remind him of Elissa... but it was a well-known fact that people were often attracted by the same particular physical type in human relationships. Why should it be anything more sinister than that? That resemblance might initially have drawn Alex's attention to her but he was far too strong a character to have married her to live out some ridiculous fantasy. Any male who would go to such lengths would be obsessed to a degree that suggested male instability. For goodness' sake, the woman had disappeared out of Alex's life thirteen years ago, turned him off love, *hurt* him! Elissa had to be more of a bad memory for Alex than a good one.

An hour later she stood in the same bedroom where she had awakened in a bower of flowers almost two months earlier. As she recalled her panic and horror that morning, it didn't seem possible that she was the same person any more. She was changing, she acknowledged; she *had* changed. In a cheval-glass, she saw a woman sheathed in an elegant Christian Lacroix dress—a woman who looked rich and exclusive and who held her head high. But the alteration was more than one of appearance and self-image. When she was with Alex, Sara realised, she felt extraordinarily free simply to be herself.

And wasn't it time that she cleared up his misapprehensions about Brian? If only Alex had not witnessed her shock and distress that day! He had seen too much, got too close. It wasn't that surprising that he should still believe that she loved Brian. Not one single thing had she done to convince him otherwise. And no, Alex was not comfortable with the belief that he was the consolation prize. A rueful smile curved her lips. She didn't blame him for lashing out at her last night. They would have to talk.

Ladymead was festooned with scaffolding and satisfyingly alive with noise and activity. The repairs and renovation work were moving right on target. There had been no major problems, nothing the architect in charge had not been able to handle. But when the current phase was over there would still be a million things to do, including decorating and furnishing. The size of the project made her head spin but Sara could hardly wait to face the challenge.

She was wandering around the kitchen when one of the workmen put his head round the door. 'There's a woman looking for you out front, Mrs Rossini!'

It was Alex's sister, Donatella. Sara stilled in momentary surprise and then walked forward smiling. 'I had no idea you were still here.'

'By the time I did my shopping, wandered round the galleries and caught up with old friends, my one-week stay easily ran over two,' Donatella admitted cheerfully.

'I saw Alex at the office and when he said you were down here I decided to join you... You don't mind?'

'I'm delighted to have the company.'

'I was dying to see it. I still can't believe my eyes. It's a wonderful old house, gloriously picturesque,' Donatella sighed appreciatively as they strolled slowly indoors. 'When Papà said that Alex had bought a ruin, we all laughed because Alex cannot bear to be uncomfortable on the domestic front. He is very spoilt that way. This dust, this dirt, this frantic upheaval would drive him crazy... but what a declaration of love that he should close his eyes to all the imperfections and buy it anyway!'

'Alex knows what I like very well.' Sara's eyes suddenly gleamed with secret amusement. Alex really hadn't needed to hedge his bets with Ladymead the day he'd proposed. She still would have married him. Perhaps it was time she told him that too. 'And he can hardly have been unaware of what was required here. The *palazzo* must require fairly constant maintenance.'

'But that's different. For Alex that is the home of his earliest memories. He uses it most. Papà rarely goes to Venice now,' Donatella said as they strolled round the echoing ground floor. 'He has never liked the *palazzo* since Alex's mother died there.'

'Did he love her so much?'

Donatella looked wry. 'He would tell you he did but then they were only together three years. I'm more cynical. With every wife but Francine he fathered another child, found his attention straying and got divorced again. I think he simply likes women too much, but he does like to think of himself as a family man.'

'His children do seem to be surprisingly close.'

'We have Alex to thank for that. He kept us all in contact with each other as we grew up... yet he had the toughest childhood. He had had three stepmothers by the time he was in his teens, none of them substitute mothers.' Donatella grimaced. 'Unfortunately for Alex, he was always very much Papà's favourite. Even my own mother resented Alex, which was sad. He was only a baby when his mother died. It was not his fault that each new wife felt insecure and then decided that her child was being passed over in his favour.'

'Maybe...maybe that's why he fell for an older woman,' Sara muttered abruptly, abstractedly. Understanding what drove Alex in all his complexity did not come easily to her. Yet she so badly wanted to know what made him the way he was: capable of such immense warmth and sensitivity and then such paradoxical and chilling coldness.

'As a mother figure?' Donatella uttered a reluctant laugh and shook her head. 'I don't think so, Sara. Elissa clung to Alex. She leant on *him*. He was by far the stronger personality.'

'What was she like?'

'As a family friend, we all liked her... That is, until she became involved with Alex.' His sister compressed her lips. 'Everyone knew she was in a lousy marriage. Her husband wasn't the faithful type and she couldn't have children. I suppose she must have been very unhappy but she never complained. She worked tirelessly for charity. She was very well-known for her good works.'

'You're describing a saint.'

'A lot of people saw her in that light, so you can imagine the shocking scandal it caused when she took off with Alex. Nobody could believe it at first but I had seen her with him...' Donatella's eyes were rueful. 'He was very mature for his age, and with Alex she was a different person. It shone out of her. She couldn't hide her love. We were all very surprised when she left Alex after her husband divorced her, but to be truthful...equally relieved.'

'Why? The age difference?'

Donatella hesitated and then sighed. 'Please don't take offence...but talking about Elissa makes me feel uncomfortable. In any case, I can only repeat gossip and my own impressions as a rather judgemental teenager. Alex has never discussed Elissa with any of us.'

Sara grimaced. 'I'm sorry...my curiosity was running away with me.'

'Why?' her companion asked bluntly. 'Why concern yourself? It was a long time ago, an episode we were all glad to forget.'

Put like that, her own insecurities seemed neurotic.

'And you have been good for my brother, Sara. I saw a change in Alex today. He's more relaxed, less distant, not so driven as he used to be. You don't seem to be aware of the miracle you have worked. None of us ever really expected Alex to marry. When you grow up as we all did in divided households, it is very hard to have faith in marriage.'

But Alex didn't have faith in marriage. Oh, he had mustered impressive enthusiasm for the institution when he'd proposed but Sara reckoned that that had been for her benefit. No, for Alex this marriage was an experiment, with Ladymead the selected site for a home-making field test. But he would not be at all surprised if the experiment failed and he would probably be equally quick to cut his losses if their relationship hit one too many obstacles. The knowledge made Sara suppress a shiver.

Alex strolled into the drawing room of the town house shortly after midnight to find Sara curled up in the corner of a sofa, surrounded by a pile of magazines. 'I thought you would be in bed. You waited up for me...'

An irrepressible grin slanted her mouth. 'Alex, you suggested I rested this afternoon so that I *wouldn't* be too tired to wait up! Or did I misinterpret my instructions?'

The faintest colour highlighted the hard slant of his cheekbones and then he laughed. 'I didn't realise I was so transparent.'

'You aren't as a rule,' she said consolingly, her softened gaze roaming over his vibrantly handsome features. 'Would you like something to eat?'

'Nothing.' He surveyed her with an intensity that made her heartbeat quicken. 'So bring me up to date on the bricks and mortar rescue mission,' he invited.

'Everything's going like clockwork.'

'When do we move?'

'That depends on how quickly I can furnish and decorate.'

'I'm amazed that you're not putting us under canvas on that field that the agent had the gross pretension to call a lawn.'

'Somehow I can't see you under canvas.' She swallowed hard and held his gaze. 'And if you don't want to live there you can sell the house when the work's finished... no hard feelings,' she asserted.

An ebony brow was elevated. 'Why?'

'I didn't decide to marry you because you promised to buy it—'

'But it helped...'

'When I was walking round Ladymead that day, I had no idea that you were about to ask me to marry you or that there was ever likely to be any possibility of it becoming my home.'

A slow smile curved his mobile mouth. 'But at least admit that you pictured some glossy magazine image of wholesome family domesticity: log fires, dogs and cats, children...'

'It seems to me that you must have been tuned into pretty much the same wavelength,' Sara protested.

'*Your* wavelength. I see smoke billowing out from inefficient chimneys, cats that scratch and dogs that bark. But that's not important if you're content. *Where* I live isn't important to me,' Alex returned with wry emphasis. 'As a child I learnt not to put down roots because whenever I did Sandro and I were on the move again. The abandoned wives and kids always got what was euphemistically termed the marital home. Becoming too comfortable or too attached to the roof over my head was never a good idea.'

The sheer physical upheaval of separation and divorce had not occurred to Sara before. Now she felt guilty. She should have appreciated that Alex had lived in many different houses throughout his childhood, never in one secure home. Had each new wife insisted on a new roof? And every time Sandro had opted for another divorce Alex's world would have been thrown into chaos again.

'While you, on the other hand...' Alex studied her with keen dark eyes. 'You grew up in a house where you were made to feel like an intruder, where nothing was ever really yours and where you felt you did not belong but where you tried very hard to fit. I can understand now why you dream of making a home that is entirely your own and why that need should be so important to you. But I have to confess that I didn't understand all that a month ago.'

And it's at times like this that *I* understand why I love you, Sara thought. Her throat had thickened. She slid upright and covered the distance between them in seconds. Alex's arms came round her and she breathed in deep. 'If the chimneys smoke, I'll get them fixed, and we'll start out with only one small pet—'

'That would be stretching self-denial too far, *cara*. The mice in that house require an army of cats.'

'Pest control, Alex...and they've already been...*three* times,' she admitted ruefully.

With a husky laugh, Alex pulled her close and looked down at her beautiful face. 'Only one warning, *bella mia*...if you ever bring a wallpaper book to bed—'

'You'll put the house on the market again?' she teased as he lifted her off her feet.

'I couldn't do that. Ladymead is yours.'

'Mine?' she said blankly.

'It's in your name. Think of it as a wedding present.'

'Are you selling this place?' she mumbled in a daze.

'Why? It's useful when I want to entertain.'

Abandoned wives always got the marital home... Was she getting hers in advance? And Alex was retaining the town house for his own use, ensuring that if they broke up he would suffer minimal inconvenience. Was it crazy of her to think like that? While she was wondering, Alex bent his dark head and exacted a long, lingering kiss that made her toes curl in wild anticipation.

Much later, lying in a wonderful tangle of peaceful satiation, Sara rubbed her cheek lovingly against a smooth brown shoulder and thought about the chaotic, insecure childhood Alex must have had. 'You're really close to your brother and sisters, aren't you?'

'It astonishes me when I think of what a whiny little brat Marco was, always throwing tantrums and telling tales,' he mused lazily. 'Donatella, now... she was very quiet and serious. She used to follow me everywhere. The twins... they were born shortly before I opted out of my father's tangled love life. Their mother was convinced I had to be pathologically jealous of them. *Dio* ... she panicked if I went near them!'

'Bitch,' Sara said feelingly.

Alex vented a wry laugh. 'She's not like that now. She hasn't remarried and she hates Francine, so if there's a problem with Cara or Lucilla it lands in my lap.'

'Why not their father's?'

'Sandro will use any excuse not to get involved, and his excuse is generally Francine. She rules him with a rod of iron. She's very conscious that she's survived longer than any of her predecessors. She's hard as nails but occasionally I feel a little sorry for her. She's thirty-seven and I strongly suspect she would like a child but she's convinced that a baby would land her in the divorce court, and, going on previous form, she's very probably right,' Alex conceded. 'Like me, Francine worked out a long time ago that Sandro finds a wife who is also a mother a decided turn-off.'

Sara had tensed. 'But you're not like that.'

'I'd be very stupid to tell you if I was,' Alex mocked.

'Alex ... be serious.'

'Why? Any prospect of us having a child is a very long way off,' he returned flatly.

Sara frowned, astonished that he could think that she had no right to the smallest input on the subject. 'How long ... is *very* long?'

Alex exhaled on an impatient hiss. 'Let me put it this way, *cara*—I have no plans to compete with your former fiancé in the fertility stakes!'

'I beg your pardon?' Sara gasped, thoroughly disconcerted by that response as she lifted herself up to look at him.

'Nor have I any intention of changing my mind in the near future.' Alex surveyed her with hard dark eyes. 'It's not a topic open to debate. Why do you think I take responsibility for birth control? I saw this threat clouding my horizon weeks ago!'

Threat? Her cheeks flamed. 'Did you indeed?'

'*Sì* ... the same second you told me that your cousin was pregnant,' Alex drawled softly. 'You are not in competition with her.'

'What on earth are you talking about? I asked a simple question,' Sara gritted defensively.

'And I gave you a simple answer. No,' Alex said emphatically. 'Sublimate your maternal urges in cats and dogs.'

Sara shifted across the bed as if she had been bitten by a rattlesnake. 'I have no idea why you had to drag Antonia into this!' Her voice shook with angry incomprehension and hurt.

Alex dimmed the lights. 'Go to sleep.'

'Don't treat me like a child!' she protested incredulously.

'I refuse to argue with you about this.'

'You're like your father, aren't you?' she condemned wildly.

'*Madre di Dio* . . . if I'd been like Sandro, *cara*, you would have been dumped before the ink was dry on the marriage licence!'

In the darkness Sara went rigid with shocked disbelief. He played really dirty in a fight. . . And you're *surprised*? an inner voice carolled drily. 'So why didn't you just do that?' she demanded.

'Don't ask me in the mood I'm in.'

'I want to know!'

'It's like there's a piece of elastic which keeps on hauling me back . . . but at this moment, *bella mia*, it's stretched very taut!' And the fact that he didn't like the feeling at all lanced clear as a bell through every splintering syllable.

'Help yourself to a pair of scissors!' Sara suggested painfully, sick and tired of the frequency with which Alex implied that their marriage might not have a future. Every time she stood up to him, he unleashed that threat.

Alex bit out a raw, exasperated imprecation in Italian. Sara pinned her tremulous mouth shut with enormous effort. There was a volcano of injustice boiling up inside her. One little question, casually asked, innocently meant—for, believe it or not, she was *not* gasping to become pregnant right at this moment—and she wouldn't have minded if Alex had merely said he would prefer to wait a year or two. Yes, she wanted Alex's baby but only when she felt secure in their relationship and only when he felt the same way. So what on earth did Antonia have to do with it? Did he really think that she would try to keep up with her cousin in such an utterly stupid way?

Or was Alex being almost too clever for his own good? she wondered painfully. Throwing up a red herring to conceal the fact that *he* didn't want children and certainly wouldn't risk an accidental pregnancy when he couldn't see their marriage lasting very long . . . was that what he had been doing? And she remembered, with bitter clarity, thinking that a woman in love with a man who did not love her might well become insecure, oversensitive and anxious. And now she knew it to be the case, Sara reflected with stricken insight.

CHAPTER NINE

'IM SORRY,' the polite female voice responded when Sara reached for the phone at almost the same moment that she woke up in bed alone. 'Mr Rossini is in conference.'

'I'm sorry,' the same infuriatingly detached tone told her an hour later. 'Mr Rossini is not presently available.

'I am so sorry,' Sara was informed shortly before lunchtime and this time the voice sounded reprovingly weary. 'Mr Rossini is airborne.'

Airborne? Staving off a ludicrous image of Alex in free flight round the office, Sara cast aside the phone. It had finally dawned on her that he hadn't put his wife's name on the shortlist of approved callers allowed instant access to him...surely a deliberate oversight? How much enough was enough?. A slow, steady anger was escalating inside Sara. She had done nothing to deserve such treatment.

He phoned from Paris at eight that evening. 'Things are hotting up here. I won't be back tonight,' he imparted. 'Everything OK?'

'Great,' Sara said in a stifled tone, for her anger had turned cold and heavy inside her.

'It might take me a couple of days to tie the loose ends up.'

'I understand.'

'I need a copy of a document on my desk in the library. Could you fax it to me?' He passed on the details in exactly the same tone that he had always utilised when she had been a humble employee. And she made a discovery there and then. Alex fell back behind that detachment instinctively when anything was wrong between them. He held her at a distance, forestalling argument or indeed any form of intimacy. No longer did she wonder why she had felt so damnably awkward with Alex on the phone before their marriage. That chill, silent disapproval could come down the line like a blast of polar snow.

Early the next morning Sara reached a very tough decision. No, Alex wasn't going to do this to her—blowing hot, blowing cold, making her feel that the smallest disagreement or displeasure might lead to the breakdown of their marriage. It was like being forced to live on a knife-edge. The more she took of it, the worse it would get. She packed a case with casual clothing. It would mean roughing it but she intended to stay at Ladymead. All she really needed for tonight was food...and a bed. So she would go shopping on the way down.

She faxed a message to Alex before she climbed into the limousine.

'Dear Alex,' it ran, 'waiting to be abandoned is bad for my nerves, so I've taken care of the problem for you. I am abandoning you.'

The builders' foreman greeted her at the door of the manor house. 'The phone has been ringing off the hook for you for the past two hours, Mrs Rossini. Somebody called Pete.'

'So, you are *there*,' Pete muttered frantically when she answered the next time the phone rang. 'What the heck was in that fax? Alex went through the roof and he was in a bad enough mood even before it arrived!'

'Did he tell you to track me down?'

'Obviously. This bid is at a crucial stage. He's very busy with the French negotiators,' Pete stressed with audible incredulity, that she should require such an explanation. 'Have you had bad news or something? Can't you handle it on your own? You know Alex doesn't like to be disturbed when he's—'

'I don't work for Alex any more,' she reminded him. 'Just tell him I was too busy to come to the phone.'

'I can't tell Alex *that*!' he spluttered in horror.

'But then Alex shouldn't have asked you to deal with this.'

In the background, she heard a deeper masculine voice intrude. There was a short silence and then, without warning, her eardrums were seared. 'What the bloody hell are you playing at?' Alex launched down the line at her full volume. 'How dare you send me a message like that?'

'That kind of blackmail doesn't exactly make your day, does it?' Sara pointed out gently.

Alex wasn't listening. 'I want you back in London by tonight!'

'No, Alex—'

'If you don't stop this insanity right now, I'll—'

'Save your breath. I know the options. Either you make a commitment to our marriage or you let me go, and since I really don't think you have the guts to do the first I'm placing my bets on the second,' Sara murmured tightly.

She replaced the receiver, her face white and stiff with strain. Then she straightened her shoulders and slowly released her breath. Now she had to wait. The next move was his to make. What she really needed, she conceded tautly, was nerves of steel, and what nerve she did have was petering out fast. She was risking so much...but *not* for so little. Would Alex come down to Ladymead? How long would it take him to come? Was she mad to have thrown down the gauntlet so blatantly?

She had taken Alex by surprise. You had to knock him off balance to make him listen. And if he left her here, chose to take her at her word—well, she was only ending what would have ended anyway, she told herself unhappily. She had to know whether or not he intended to give their marriage a chance. From the outside it didn't look as though he did. If she crossed him, he closed her out and put as much distance between them as he could. And maybe if he had loved her she could have handled that better, practised patience and hoped that time would take care of the problem.

But Alex didn't love her. Even worse he disliked the idea that she had any sort of power over him, even if it was only the far from cerebral power of sex. All the control had to be on his side...just as it had been in Venice. The expert lover and the amateur. Alex had controlled everything they'd shared. She sensed that it had always been like that for him with women. He had to call every shot. He didn't compromise. And he didn't trust her either.

By mid-afternoon the bed that she had purchased had been delivered. For the first time in her life, Sara had employed cash as an inducement to better service. She couldn't say that she was proud of herself but she could live with it when the alternative was sleeping on the floor. Ladymead was empty by four. The workforce downed tools and took off. Sara was left alone, free to wander silent rooms and wonder how she would furnish them, but the moment she appreciated that Alex might never share the house with her any interest she might have had drained away.

Almost as quickly she began to doubt and question her own actions. Wasn't it very probable that Alex would see her behaviour as a selfish, immature demand for attention? Suddenly she could not picture him responding to her change of abode with anything other than exasperated silence. Give her enough rope and let her hang herself with it—she could imagine Alex thinking like that. She had been the one to walk out; let her be the one to dig herself out of the tight corner she had put herself in. And that was assuming that Alex didn't decide just to let her go...

Suddenly she saw that, while she had very real concerns about their relationship, challenging Alex to such a degree had been needlessly provocative. Shouldn't she have tried harder to cut across those barriers of his to tell him without anger that they had to talk openly and honestly?

It was getting dark when she made herself sandwiches and then looked at them without appetite. The rain had come on slowly in a soft mist that dampened and blurred the windows. Now hailstones were lashing the panes. The electricity was only on in part of the house. As the shadows lengthened, she negotiated the magnificent main staircase with care, grateful that she had bought a torch. She crossed creaking floorboards in the bedroom that she had selected because it was next to the one functioning bathroom. Eventually she stopped pacing and wished that she had brought something to read with her. Shortly after ten she climbed into bed to keep warm while she listened to the rain and the wind battering the house.

A distant thumping noise woke her up at some timeless stage of the night. For a minute she was completely disorientated and then recall returned, making her spring out of her bed, breathlessly locate the light switch and lift the torch. It was almost two in the morning. From the top of the stairs, she could see the sturdy front door shuddering in complaint on its wrought-iron hinges and hurried down.

'What did I do in my last life to deserve this?' Alex splintered savagely as he rammed the door back in his eagerness to get over the threshold and out of the howling wind and rain.

Sara fell back, momentarily astonished by his appearance. He was soaked to the skin, his suit plastered to every muscular line of his powerful frame. He looked as if he had been swimming fully clothed, but he was not only very wet, he was also very dirty: mud was caked on his shoes and trousers and the front of a once pristine white shirt where he had clearly wiped his hands.

'If this is country life, you can bloody well keep it!' he blistered, fixing outraged golden eyes on her. 'The Bugatti died in a flood down that hellish mud track!'

'Oh, dear...' Sara said in a wobbly undertone, watching him rake a shaking hand through his wet, curling hair, pushing it back off his forehead as he stood there dripping, and she had a truly terrifying urge to put both arms round him and soothe him as if he were a furious, frustrated little boy who had just discovered the awful truth that life didn't always go his way.

'I need a bath and a drink.'

'Oh, dear...' Sara said again helplessly, knowing that neither was available and not quite sure how to break such bad news.

'My case is still in the car!' Alex delivered between clenched teeth.

'Oh, dear...' It was hard to think of anything more positive to say.

'*Madre di Dio*...if you say that once more...!' he exploded, but at the same time he shivered convulsively.

And it was the shiver that unfroze Sara. 'You need to get out of those clothes. Come upstairs.'

'The helicopter couldn't fly in the storm,' Alex grated, still boiling with rage as he followed her up the stairs. 'The jet was delayed. And there's not even electric light here. Have you any idea how long I've been banging at that door?'

Sara threw open the door of the bathroom, switching on the mercifully working light with a flourish. 'There's no hot water but everything else functions,' she told him encouragingly.

'No hot water?' Alex whispered in stunned disbelief.

Sara gave him a gentle push over the threshold and closed the door on him. Then she thought fast. In minutes she was fully dressed again. Lifting the torch and pulling on a jacket, she left the house.

It was a wild night and the sky was as black as pitch. The drive, with its potholes the size of craters, was a disaster zone for anyone forced to negotiate it without light. Alex's car had died near the very foot where the drive disappeared altogether as it dipped suddenly beneath a large, dark, uninviting expanse of water. Thankfully, Alex hadn't locked his car as he should have done. She waded in and located his leather case, searched for the keys and assumed that he had taken them with him. It was a good half-mile trudge back to the house but the rain was slackening off and the wind was dying down.

Alex had come. Alex had actually made a big effort to come. She hadn't expected him tonight, not so soon. And she certainly hadn't expected him to show up in the early hours, wet and filthy, a far cry from his usual immaculately groomed self. She had wanted very badly to laugh once the shock had worn off but amusement would have been cruel when Alex was so clearly at the end of his tether. A lukewarm shower would be equally cruel, she reflected. Maybe she should have offered to boil the kettle for him... What a shame she had switched the heater off earlier when she couldn't quite work out how to set the time switch.

When she found the bathroom deserted, she thrust the case through the bedroom door like a sneak thief. She didn't look in. 'I'll make you some coffee!' she called winningly, and hurriedly escaped again.

She carefully washed the beaker that she had used earlier and wished that she hadn't been quite so ridiculously sparing in what she had brought for her own needs. She could offer him a biscuit, a cup of instant coffee and banana sandwiches—not exactly a feast for a male with a healthy appetite.

'You shouldn't have gone back to the car for me...but thanks. The gesture was appreciated.'

Sara spun round. Alex was standing in the doorway wearing a black Armani sweater and well-cut linen trousers. He looked heart-stoppingly gorgeous. Her ribcage felt constrained. 'It was the least I could do. Anyway I had a torch.'

'This place is a hell-hole. And it's a judgement on me,' Alex mused fatalistically, scanning the vast, comfortless kitchen with a barely concealed shudder. 'I knew what I was doing. I disobeyed my own instincts—'

'Coffee?' Sara suggested, setting the beaker on the long, scrubbed table. 'Banana sandwiches are all I can offer in the way of food, I'm afraid.'

Alex didn't move. He exhaled sharply and surveyed her in grim silence for a long moment. 'Maybe you'd like to tell me what the hell all this is about...?'

Sara flushed uncomfortably. His anger vented, he now sounded coolly reasonable. 'I'm sorry you had such a rough time getting here—'

'Stick to the point.'

Sara stiffened. 'I had no idea you would come here tonight.'

'I very nearly didn't,' Alex admitted. 'Intelligence told me to leave you here to stew.'

'But you didn't...'

'No, rage blew me in with the storm. There was also the natural concern that something had happened that I didn't know about...some highly mysterious event which would miraculously justify your behaviour.' Alex regarded her with hard challenge. 'And if you can't come up with that miracle I'm calling a car and going back to London.'

'You see? You're doing it again,' Sara responded tautly. 'You're threatening me; you do it all the time—'

'I don't threaten you,' Alex countered fiercely.

'Maybe you don't even realise you're doing it, maybe it's second nature.' Beneath her bright, anxious eyes, her cheeks were taut with stress. 'But you do it. If I annoy you, Alex, you immediately close me out and start telling me that our marriage is on borrowed time if I continue. You enforce conversational no-go areas—'

'That is nonsense,' Alex interposed in flat rebuttal.

She was holding herself so rigid that her muscles ached with strain. 'No, it isn't—'

'*Dio*...' Shimmering eyes whipped over her with scorching incredulity. 'You *fax* me the news that you're leaving me! You drag me all the way from Paris on a fool's errand by crying wolf and then think you can tell me I deserved this childish charade?'

'I wanted you to know what emotional blackmail feels like,' Sara admitted with helpless honesty. 'You use it on me and it makes me angry too. I don't like having my strings pulled either. I don't like the fact that you make me scared to talk about things we need to talk about. I don't like being judged and refused the right to defend myself...'

Suddenly his glittering gaze pierced her like an arrow finding its target. '*Madre di Dio*...you did *all* this purely because I refused to consider allowing you to become pregnant?' he demanded in outrage.

Sara flinched in disbelief and then her chin came up, her hands knotting into frustrated fists as her temper rose to the fore. 'I think I'd have to be a mental case to want your baby, Alex! Not only would you not want the child, I would undoubtedly be left to raise it on my own, and believe me, at twenty-three, with my whole life ahead of me, I have no plans to shoot myself in the foot! No intelligent woman would choose to bring a child into an unstable relationship, most especially not when her partner has made his negative attitude resoundingly clear—'

'We do not have an unstable relationship, and I'm not your partner. I'm your husband,' Alex grated with an irrelevance which merely increased her anger.

'Furthermore, I bitterly resent the suggestion that I couldn't be trusted not to become *accidentally* pregnant! How dare you compare me to Antonia?' Sara asked him furiously, well into her stride now. 'I wouldn't trick any man like that—'

'You wanted *his* child,' Alex interposed icily.

Her head swam. Nothing that she was trying to spell out seemed to be getting through. Alex was missing the point... or possibly she was missing his, but what mattered most to Sara at that moment was that Alex should understand that he had misjudged her and, in so doing, caused her a great deal of pain. 'That was different...'

'Patently.'

Momentarily Sara closed her eyes, needing to get a grip on her anger, knowing that this was not the discussion she had planned. Slowly she breathed in. 'It was a different sort of relationship,' she proffered. 'Brian and I...we were more friends than lovers. We shared a lot of interests. We had the same goals. Brian likes to feel secure, so do I. We agreed about so many things—'

'How touching.'

'What I'm trying to explain is that wanting children was just part of that.' Sara shrugged a shoulder and was briefly silent while she thought back. 'We had our whole future mapped out and it felt very safe, and maybe we both got a bit smug about how well matched we were... and maybe I did get so carried away organising everything that I wouldn't have noticed if he had six Antonias on the side!'

'You loved him,' Alex murmured harshly.

Sara lowered her head and wondered. Had she ever really loved Brian? She believed that she had been very, very fond of him but Brian had never had the power to tear her heart out as Alex did. There had been no highs, no lows, no soul-stirring fear or excitement. Two lonely people had met and formed a mutual support system which they had called love for want of a better word. 'Not as much as I thought I did. You were right about that,' she conceded wryly, her face pensive. 'Three years ago Brian wanted Antonia but she wasn't interested then—'

'He didn't belong to you.'

'No, it wasn't only that.' Sara wanted to be fair to her cousin. 'Back then, Antonia's modelling career looked like it was heading straight to the top. She was mixing with a lot of exciting people, travelling the world, having a fabulous time. She was only twenty-one, too. My uncle and aunt may have spoilt her to death but they also landed her with a whole set of gilt-edged expectations to live up to. She was the family star. They expected her to become a supermodel and marry someone...' her soft mouth curved with rueful amusement ' ... someone like you. I don't think I can blame her for not noticing Brian in those days.'

'What a very generous outlook you have.' Alex's dark gaze rested intently on her taut profile.

'No, I don't. I confess to feeling secretly pleased when her modelling career slid downhill again. She's very good at putting people's backs up. When she got into debt last year, she had to sell her apartment and her parents naturally assumed I would share my flat with her. When I think about it, Antonia's had a tough time, yet Brian was always sniping at her, running her down because she hurt his ego. I should have seen that, recognised it for what it was—'

'Fatal attraction,' Alex interposed flatly. 'There whether you want it to be or not.'

She wanted to be brave enough to ask if that was how Alex felt about her but she couldn't bring herself to plunge that deep. It wasn't a good idea to ask a question if you thought you might crumble when you got the answer, she thought strickenly. 'Brian thought he couldn't have her, so he settled for me.' She swallowed hard in the throbbing silence. 'I don't love him any more, Alex.'

His strong dark features were harshly set. 'You don't need to say that, Sara.'

'You see?' she demanded abruptly, her eyes flaring. 'You're doing it again. You're refusing to accept what I say. Perhaps there's a part of you which feels happier thinking I'm still in love with Brian!'

'That's a ridiculous suggestion—'

'Is it? I'm not so sure. Out of bed,' Sara framed tightly, 'you like a certain safe, emotional distance, don't you? All the boundaries are yours. You can barely mention the fact that we're married without implying that it's not likely to last...but that it's going to be all my fault if it doesn't!'

A dark rise of blood stained his hard cheekbones.

'It makes me feel like I'm waiting for a redundancy notice, and when I phone you at the office and I can't even get to speak to you I feel like I've already been dumped!'

'What are you talking about?'

'You didn't put my name on the list, did you?' Sara accused him.

'*Dio*...of course I didn't—you're my wife!' Alex gritted. 'Are you telling me that that stupid girl didn't put your calls through?'

Sara's mouth opened and shut again. It had never occurred to her that her inability to get Alex at the end of a phone line might simply be the result of human error.

'So I have her to thank for that fax!' Alex was visibly enraged by the idea.

'I assumed that she was doing what she had been told to do.'

'I am such an ignorant boor that I would tell an employee that I will not take calls from my own wife?'

Sara reddened hotly. 'Well, no, but—'

'*Grazie, cara*...what a wonderful light I appear to you in!'

'You can't blame me for assuming—' she began defensively.

'Can't I?' Alex shot her a look of derision. 'Was it totally beyond your power to insist on speaking to me? Is it my fault you let yourself be repulsed by a little office girl?'

Sara's cat-green eyes glittered. 'Probably. On the phone you treat me as if I'm *still* "a little office girl". I wouldn't have been too sure of my ground had I chosen to insist. The impression I receive is...' she hesitated and then forced herself on '...is that marriage was a step too far for you.'

Alex's facial muscles had clenched hard. 'I never thought you would force a confrontation like this.'

'You didn't leave me with much choice. I'm not like you,' Sara confided shakily. 'I can't shove things under the carpet and pretend they didn't happen the way you do. I can't behave normally when you freeze me off. I get angry and I get hurt. I've never known anyone who can be so warm...and then so cold...'

Alex was very still and very pale beneath his year-round tan.

'I mean—' Sara gulped, her throat closing over, knowing that she had dived into deeper waters than she had ever envisaged, but somehow unable to stop herself. 'When you called me from Paris, Alex...I knew you were just delighted to be away from me—'

'It wasn't like that,' he countered fiercely, his graceful hands restively clenching and then digging into the pockets of his tailored trousers, pulling the fine fabric taut over his long, powerful thighs.

But he still wasn't going to tell her how it *had* been, she registered painfully. 'What I'm trying to ask is, did you ever plan for this marriage to be a real one...or was it just a manipulative game which got out of hand?

You knew exactly what you had to say to persuade me to marry you but how much of it did you actually mean? If you're having regrets already, it would be kinder simply to be honest.'

Alex released his breath in a sudden hiss. He looked like someone being subjected to some highly sophisticated form of invisible torture. 'I don't have any regrets—'

'But you don't trust me.'

'I've never trusted any woman!' he bit out.

Her throat constricted. 'Alex, I'd need lessons to be one tenth as naturally devious as you are. What have you got to worry about?'

He stared back at her with fathomless eyes as dark as ebony. 'I don't want to lose you. You're very important to me, *cara*.'

It was the most complimentary thing that Alex had ever said to her that did not relate to sex. She breathed again, a wave of dizziness which she recognised as intense relief sweeping over her, leaving her light-headed.

'I wasn't aware that I was making you feel threatened,' he conceded in a driven undertone. 'But this kind of communication doesn't come easily to me. In fact, the more I feel, the less I want to talk about it.'

As her gaze collided with his rather grim half-smile of self-awareness, her heart flipped a somersault behind her breastbone. She wanted to be in his arms but instead she turned away and asked him prosaically if he wanted anything to eat.

And suddenly Alex was laughing and the tension, still humming uneasily in the atmosphere, evaporated simultaneously. 'You know, *bella mia*, if I'd arrived here to candlelight and a champagne reception, I'd have been outraged.'

'You would have felt set up.'

'But there is such a thing as a happy medium,' Alex imparted with the unevenness of amusement tugging at his dark deep voice.

'Like a hot bath and a drink?'

'Banana sandwiches?' He repeated her earlier offer, shaking his darkly handsome head. 'I haven't had them since I was a child. Marcella used to make them for me.'

And while she made the sandwiches he talked about the *palazzo* housekeeper with a warmth that eventually made her eyes burn. She had noticed Alex's fondness for the older woman in Venice, hadn't really thought about it much. But now she saw a lonely, loving little boy, starved of affection by a succession of indifferent stepmothers, and with a father who was very charming and no doubt very proud of his eldest son but far too selfish to have made any attempt to give him a stable home life. Alex knew far more than she did about feeling like an outsider. That was why he had so easily understood her own insecurities.

Dawn was breaking when they finally made it to bed. 'I need to get the Bugatti moved,' Alex groaned.

'It's Saturday,' she reminded him. 'It won't matter if the drive's blocked but you should have locked it up.'

'What with? I fell getting out of the car. I dropped the keys and my mobile phone in that filthy water!'

'Oh, dear.' But she giggled this time when she said it.

Alex hauled her down on top of him. 'You are the only woman I ever got my feet dirty for.'

'And you looked so funny!'

'And never felt less like laughing,' he admitted. 'It was not quite the entrance I had planned.'

'But I was terribly impressed by it all the same. I was struck dumb.'

Alex curved a hungry hand round the pouting swell of one bare breast, centring every nerve-ending in her thrumming body on one hot spot, and she ran out of oxygen all in one go, shaken by the sheer intensity of

her response. 'I'm feeling very encouraged, *bella mia*.
This is another first. No nightgown,' he teased.

Perhaps not so strange an oversight. It was wonderful
what increased security did for your confidence, Sara
mused. Only now did she see that their marriage was as
real and as important to Alex as it had always been to
her.

'Yours?' From the doorstep, Janice Dalton scrutinised
the cream Jaguar with its scarlet leather upholstery and
her mouth compressed. 'Very ostentatious...'

Sara reddened slightly. 'Alex bought it for my birthday.
I was disappointed that you couldn't join us for dinner.'

'I'm afraid we'd already made other arrangements.'

Sara was shown into the lounge. Her determined smile
revealed nothing of her uneasiness. Over the past month
the Daltons had turned down her every invitation to visit.
She had been relieved when her aunt had phoned her
and asked her over but there was a marked coolness in
the older woman's manner. What on earth was wrong?
Sara wondered anxiously.

'I might as well get right to the heart of the matter,'
her aunt told her stiffly. 'Antonia and Brian have split
up.'

Sara tensed. 'I'm sorry.'

'I wonder if you really are?' A flush had mottled the
older woman's cheeks.

'Yes,' Sara said quietly. 'I am sorry.'

Her aunt gave her an angry look. 'Of course you can
afford to be gracious. You've done very well out of all
this. Heaven knows, I never thought to see *you* swanning
up in a brand-new Jaguar, dressed like Princess Diana!'

'Alex likes me to look smart.' And I will not tell him
about this when I go home, she reflected painfully. It
was uncanny how often Alex was right about people.
Her aunt couldn't hide her resentment that Sara had

married a very rich and powerful man, while her adored daughter had married a relatively ordinary one.

'Brian's been very cruel to Antonia.'

'I don't think this is any of my business.'

'That's the trouble...it's very much your business!' Janice Dalton condemned. 'Brian told Antonia that he's still in love with you!'

Sara was taken aback by the angry assurance until it occurred to her that it was probably something that Brian had thrown out in an argument. She had known that her cousin and her former fiancé would have a stormy relationship. Brian had very fixed ideas about the sort of wife he wanted and by no stretch of the imagination was Antonia likely to fulfil a stay-at-home role. Antonia didn't cook, didn't clean and sulked if she sat in more than one night a week.

'I don't believe for one minute that Brian still loves me,' Sara retorted. 'In fact I doubt that he ever did.'

'Antonia's had a terrible time.' Visibly mollified by Sara's assurance, her aunt began spilling out a highly coloured account of Antonia's sufferings—how Brian had demanded that they live in the house which *Sara* had furnished, how mean he was with money, how selfish, how insensitive...

'In fact what Brian badly needs is someone to talk some sense into him!' her aunt completed, tight-mouthed. 'He wouldn't listen to me but he might listen to you.'

Sara froze. '*Me*...talk to Brian?' she whispered in disbelief.

'Brian and you were always good friends. Why shouldn't you speak to him?'

'But I—'

'After all, Brian and Antonia only had a harmless little flirtation and then *you* rushed off and got involved with Alex Rossini. Let's face it, you weren't interested in having Brian back then! You couldn't have cared less.

It's time that Brian heard that from you and stopped throwing you up to Antonia! Believe me, I don't like having to ask you for help,' the older woman informed her bitterly, resentfully, 'but I think you could get through to Brian where nobody else can.'

'I'm sorry, but I don't want to interfere and Antonia would be furious, and rightfully so, if I did.' Sara stood up.

'You're being very selfish, Sara. You wouldn't be where you are now if it hadn't been for this family's generosity!' Janice Dalton shot at her in furious reproach. 'I wonder how much interest Alex Rossini would have had in you if you'd been brought up in some council home?'

Sara had lost all her natural colour. It shook her that her aunt could cruelly throw that debt in her face. Over the years Sara had always shown her gratitude. But maybe she *was* being selfish. All that crossed her mind was that to meet Brian she would have to lie to Alex because Alex would never agree to such a meeting. Alex was extremely possessive...

'You owe it to me to do whatever you can to help,' the older woman spelt out harshly. 'Antonia need never know.'

'And then I melt back out of your lives again...right?'

For the first time Janice Dalton looked embarrassed.

'That's all right. Alex is all the family I need.'

'Sara...'

But Sara walked away, knowing that she would never walk willingly back into that house again. She wasn't wanted there. The little orphaned niece whom the Daltons had so generously taken into their home had committed the unforgivable sin of obscuring the family star in terms of material advancement. Sara felt slightly sick.

Further down the street she parked the car and lifted the mobile phone. Get this over with, she urged herself when she hesitated. *What Alex doesn't know about won't hurt him. This isn't going to hurt anyone. Aunt Janice is right. If there is any possibility that you could help, you should try.* She called Brian at work.

'What do you want?' he snapped.

A wry smile touched her strained mouth. Hardly the response of a man in love, she thought.

'You've heard about Toni and me, haven't you?' he assumed peevishly.

'Do you want to talk about it?'

'Why should you care?' Brian demanded bitterly.

'Once we were good friends. It might help if we talked.'

'I don't see how...but why not?' he muttered in a self-pitying tone.

She agreed to meet him after work at the house. Evidently her cousin had refused to live there and Brian had moved in alone. She was sitting in a traffic jam when Alex phoned.

'How did it go with your aunt?' he enquired straight off.

Her stomach twisted with guilt when she thought of the lie she was about to tell. Shakily she breathed in. 'I'll be back late. I've actually just popped out for a few messages. My aunt's invited over some friends and I promised to stay for the evening,' she said stiltedly.

There was a long pause.

'No problems, then?'

She bit her lower lip and tasted blood. 'Well, my aunt's a bit cool—'

'The friends don't include Brian, do they?'

Sara almost choked. 'Of course not!'

'Just checking, *bella mia*. You sound upset. Why don't you develop a headache and bow out? I was planning to finish early tonight.'

Her eyes burned. 'I'll be home as soon as I can.'

'You stay under the speed limit. No racing,' Alex warned. 'I want you back all in one healthy piece, Signora Rossini.'

The constrictions in her throat ballooned. 'Yes ... Sorry, the traffic's very heavy. I have to go now ...'

Damn Brian and Antonia, she reflected with sudden, desperate resentment. It was one thing to wish them well, quite another to get involved to the extent of being forced to lie to Alex. But then she should have told the truth and faced the music. She was a lousy liar. And Alex was so attuned to her emotions now that he picked up on her tensions. She had this awful feeling that she was going to have to tell him anyway. And that would cause trouble. Lying had only made it worse, she saw now, and writhed with guilt.

Brian was waiting for her. Sara tried not to stare at the wallpaper half-ripped off the wall in the hall. 'Toni,' Brian said succinctly.

'You can't blame her for not wanting to live here. In every way that matters, I made this *my* house.'

'I blame her for everything.'

'It takes two people to have an affair.'

'But it only takes one liar to force an affair into a shotgun marriage!' Brian stabbed back bitterly. 'She told me she was pregnant ... she's not! She was lying and I was the mug who believed her!'

Sara sank down on a sofa in the small sitting room and suddenly understood a great deal. For the second time that day she was forced to listen to a catalogue of woes, this time from Brian's side of the fence. She had some sympathy for him but she didn't let it show. She let him vent the worst of his spleen, knowing that it would cool him down. 'Had it ever occurred to you that she must love you an awful lot?' she asked when he'd finally finished.

'The only person Toni loves is herself.'

'She deceived you and that was wrong but she must have been desperate for you to marry her.'

'You would never have done anything like that.'

'Brian... Antonia and I are chalk and cheese and always will be, but don't forget that it was Antonia you really wanted.'

'That's not true...'

'Be honest with yourself. She didn't suit you as well as I did but you never stopped being attracted to her. Reminding her of me isn't fair. Where is she now?'

'Staying with a friend. I told her I wanted a divorce...'

'But you don't want one, do you? You only want to punish her,' Sara guessed, and watched him redden. 'Don't you think you could give her another chance?'

'Why should I?'

'It's up to you. But Antonia won't wait forever and she won't crawl. She was very hurt when you didn't stand by her after I found the two of you together. That was the time when you should have admitted how you really felt about her. She was afraid that you and I would get back together again. I'm sure that's the only reason she lied and pretended to be pregnant.'

Well over an hour later Sara climbed back into her car. She was exhausted and she had talked herself hoarse but only time would tell whether she had done any good. At least Brian had been a lot less bitter when she'd left him.

It was a long drive back down to Ladymead. She thought about Alex all the way and hoped that he wouldn't lose his temper when she admitted that she had been with Brian.

The manor house was all lit up. Alex's chauffeur was putting a case in the boot of the limousine. Sara frowned slightly. She found Alex in the spacious library which he used as an office. He was slinging files into a box. She paused on the threshold. 'What are you doing?'

Alex lifted his dark head, ice-cold eyes landing on her in glancing assault. His strong features clenched cruelly hard, his mouth flattening. 'I'm leaving you,' he said.

CHAPTER TEN

DEVASTATED by the announcement, Sara stared back at him in wide-eyed disbelief.

'In pursuit of points for being a supportive husband, I decided to join the surprise family gathering you mentioned,' Alex drawled with lethal effect.

Sara turned white with shock.

'Your uncle told me *when* you had left and while we were having a cosy little chat on the doorstep he also passed on the news that the other marriage in the family had broken up and that your aunt was upset. He hoped I would understand that he couldn't invite me indoors.'

Sara was trembling, her family's rudeness to Alex only another thorn in her shrinking flesh. She licked her dry lips. 'Alex, I can explain—'

'I know where you've been. You've been with *him* all evening,' Alex delivered with seething bite. 'The minute you found out that he was free again you betrayed yourself!'

'It wasn't like that!' she protested shakily. 'My aunt asked me to—'

'You lied to me.'

'Yes...but—'

'Did you actually make it into bed with him?' Alex demanded, a vicious edge to the sudden, slashing demand as his shimmering golden eyes cut into her. '*Dio* did I transform you into a sexually confident woman for *his* benefit?'

'Don't be disgusting!' Sara gasped.

'I find it even more disgusting that you've most probably been sitting holding hands and mumbling sweet nothings! That turns my stomach!' Alex roared back at her full-blast. 'I could understand a sexual obsession even if I couldn't condone it...but this nauseating sentimental attachment of yours makes my flesh creep—especially when I think of what you were doing with *me* in bed last night!'

Hectic pink brightened her pallor. 'You've got it all wrong!' She heard the pure panic fracturing her own voice. 'My aunt asked me to talk to Brian. I knew you wouldn't want me to and I didn't want to either but I didn't have the guts to say no when she put the pressure on. I don't feel anything for Brian any more...honestly I don't! Nothing happened, not a word was said which you could object to!'

'You lied to me—'

'I'm sorry but I was a coward. I thought I could see Brian without you ever knowing about it,' she admitted in a desperate rush. 'I just didn't want to spoil things. We've been so happy and I couldn't face another argument over him.'

'You're wasting your breath, Sara.' Alex sent her a look of cold hatred and contempt which made her reel back from him in shock. 'I'm still leaving.'

'Please listen to me...please, Alex! Brian means nothing to me—'

'No, obviously all this means slightly more to you than he does.' Alex indicated the Gothic magnificence of the room, his hard mouth twisting with bitter scorn. 'Why else would you have lied to protect yourself?'

'Because I *love* you!'

Alex gave a harsh laugh of incredulity. 'You bitch,' he breathed rawly, sweeping up the box in one powerful hand and striding past her.

Sara chased after him in despair. 'I mean it. I do love you!' she shouted after him, the words echoing through the great hall and coming back to her with an eerie resonance.

Alex swung back, his cheekbones fiercely prominent, the pallor beneath his sun-bronzed skin accentuating the cold austerity of his dark eyes. 'You don't know the first thing about love, *cara*. You never did,' he derided in a sudden savage undertone. He flung her a scorching look of violent threat. 'There's no way I'll agree to a divorce. I'll keep you tied to me for years and if you ever dare to bring him into this house I'll beat the hell out of the snivelling little jerk!'

Late the next morning, Sara woke up from an uneasy doze, stiff and cold. She was lying face down on the bed, still fully dressed. She focused on the crumpled white shirt lying half beneath her. Alex's shirt, still redolent of him, retrieved from the laundry like some comforting but empty talisman. Her throat ached more than ever. She faced reality. It was all her own fault, she conceded wretchedly. How could she have been that stupid!

Until yesterday she had existed in a blissful glow of contentment. They had moved into Ladymead a fortnight ago in spite of the fact that work was still continuing in various corners. Alex had taken the inconvenience in his stride. He had begun to take a tentative interest in the improvements being made, occasionally making his own suggestions. He had twice accompanied her to Sotheby's to buy furniture. They had spent last weekend on the yacht and she had discovered that she liked sailing and didn't get sick. Indeed the only time she ever felt tense with Alex was when she found herself having to swallow back words of love.

So what had she thought she would achieve by telling him that she loved him last night? Right at the beginning, Alex had made it clear that he didn't want her love...but after their wedding he had made it even more clear that he could not stand the idea of Brian having her love either. In fact, he couldn't even tolerate the mention of Brian's name without becoming aggressive, derisive or broodingly silent. Jealousy, she thought dazedly—rampant, murderous jealousy, not just arrogant male possessiveness, not just hostility to the idea that her loyalties might be divided. In Venice she should have had greater faith in her own suspicions. Had she understood, would she have been more honest last night?

In lying she had dug her own grave with Alex. She had lied on impulse, choosing what had seemed an easy way out of a difficult situation. Her primary motivation had been the need not to cause trouble in her own marriage. But how on earth could she persuade Alex to trust her again after what she had done? How could she ever convince him that she loved and needed *him*, not his wealth or any other man? Well, certainly not by sitting feeling sorry for herself in yesterday's clothes with eyes as red as overripe tomatoes! came back the answer.

When she went downstairs, she looked into the library, for the first time really taking in the devastation which Alex had wreaked the previous night. Filing drawers and cupboard doors hung open. Books and papers were tumbled across the desktop, with many more on the floor. Alex was a formidably tidy individual in any working environment. And yet last night he had torn this immaculately organised room apart and ended up only removing a single, half-empty box.

Had she arrived home earlier than he had expected? Something told her that had she returned a couple of hours later Alex would by then have swept the boards of Ladymead so clean of his presence that she would have had trouble finding evidence that he had *ever* lived here with her. It was a chilling thought, emphasising the frightening speed with which Alex had decided to walk out on their marriage. An instantaneous decision, immediately acted upon.

Instinctively she began to return the library carefully to order, and then slowly her hands fell still again. *Alex wasn't coming back.* Alex wasn't coming back unless she kidnapped him. She had given him the true story last night and he hadn't believed her. She had told him that she loved him and he hadn't believed that either. The best she could do now was to face him again and repeat exactly the same things. So why was she wasting time cleaning up?

'Don't bother to ring ahead and warn him,' Sara told Gina, the receptionist, pleasantly on her way past. 'I want to surprise him.'

'Hello, Sara...' Pete stopped dead on the threshold of his office. 'Is Alex expecting you?'

'Do I need an appointment now, Pete?' Fevered tension made Sara sharp. She flushed. 'Sorry. Is anyone with him?'

'No, but the helicopter's waiting to take him up north.'

'I won't keep him long.'

She walked into Alex's office on the power of one long, pent-up breath.

He was standing by the windows. He spun lithely round and stilled, his strong features freezing into impassivity. Cold dark eyes settled on her without any perceptible emotion. That scared her, wiped out her prepared speech.

'Now *this* I didn't expect,' Alex drawled reflectively. 'I assumed you would have too much pride to create a scene here.'

'I'm not going to create any kind of scene...' Her heartbeat thundered in her ears as she stared back at him with a compulsive intensity that she couldn't control. Already she felt as though he had left her at least a month ago. An agonising sense of loss engulfed her without warning.

'But you shouldn't be here. I made my wishes very clear last night. Go home. You can have nothing to say that I am prepared to listen to.'

'But you *have* to listen,' Sara protested.

'Why? I don't want you anywhere near me.'

Her colour receded. On the drive up to London she had not prepared herself for this level of cruelty. Had Alex still been seething with anger, she could have borne it better, but rejection couched in cold detachment was infinitely more final. 'Alex ... haven't you ever done anything you're ashamed of "on the spur of the moment"?' she prompted in desperation.

'Married you.'

Sara flinched as if he had struck her. 'Don't do this to us. Once you said to me, "Nobody's perfect," and I know that you have a right to be angry—'

'I am not angry.' But for an instant she saw a flash of stark, bitter pain in his narrowed gaze before he screened it. 'And you're embarrassing me,' he continued with cutting precision.

In a numb motion, Sara shook her head, wondering if she had imagined that pain. 'Alex?'

He shrugged back a white shirt-cuff to scrutinse his watch. 'I haven't got time for this—'

'If you say one more word, I may well hate you for the rest of my life,' Sara told him strickenly.

'Anything you feel you have to say, share it with your lawyer, not with me.' Alex strode past her to the door.

'I thought you didn't want a divorce,' she muttered unsteadily.

'I've changed my mind,' he imparted without turning round. 'I want you out of my life.'

As the door closed Sara was in such a daze that she slid down on the nearest seat, her stomach cramping up. Oh, you really made him listen, didn't you? Oh, you were really convincing, weren't you? she derided herself. But it had been as though Alex had retreated somewhere where she couldn't reach him.

'Sara?'

She glanced up to find Marco standing several feet away. She hadn't even heard the door open.

'What did you do to my brother?' he enquired with unhidden aggression.

'Where did you come from?' she mumbled.

'I was calling in to see how he was but I appear to have missed him. So what did you do?' he demanded again fiercely. 'He came round to my apartment last night and sat there like he'd been hit by a truck!'

'Did he?' She realised how low she had sunk when she experienced a flicker of hope.

'I could see he was hurting but not a blasted word could I get out of the stubborn bastard!' Marco complained. 'So what's going on?'

'I told him a lie about something and he assumed the worst and walked out.'

'And you're surprised?'

She sighed. 'You couldn't say anything to me that would make me feel any worse than I already feel...OK?'

'I don't like seeing my brother upset like that. It would be much more healthy if he got drunk and punched walls instead of walking about like the living dead!'

Sara took a deep breath. 'Could you find out where he's gone?'

Marco walked to the door and bawled, 'Pete!'

'The Lake District,' Pete supplied cheerfully, walking in, obviously having been listening.

'What the blazes is he doing there?' Marco enquired.

'Visiting friends, I assume. He goes up there maybe twice a year. I've never gone along.'

'So?' Marco pressed impatiently. 'Who are they?'

'I spoke to the woman once. Her name's Elissa,' Pete informed them helpfully. 'I don't think I ever got her surname.'

Marco looked stunned. *'Elissa?'* he repeated. 'Are you sure?'

The roof had fallen in round Sara's head. Shock was roaring through her in waves. Pete frowned in bemusement at them both as he walked back out again.

'Did you know about this?' Marco asked her sharply. 'That Alex was in touch with her again...I mean that he even knew where she was?'

'No.'

'Elissa living in England,' he muttered, still struggling with his own incredulity. 'And he never said a word.'

'I understood she was always too special to talk about.' Sara's voice quivered.

'If you're thinking that Alex is keeping a mistress he only sees twice a year, your head's away!'

'Is it?' She studied her feverishly linked hands through a blinding blur of tears.

'Alex is nuts about you—'

'He's never said so.'

'So he's a bit tight with the words!' Marco conceded in frustration. 'But he married you. He's living in a freezing cold house with one bathroom for your benefit. He's doing weird things like buying furniture and taking off out of the office in the middle of the day... This is not Alex as we have known him for the past thirty-four years!'

'No?'

'Sara, he's so sickeningly happy with you that he throws your name into every other sentence. Pete can't keep him in the office after five. This is a guy who cannot wait to get home to his wife every night. I ask you, is it likely he's doing a line with some old doll from his past?'

'I think I'd like to meet that old doll before I commit myself,' Sara admitted as she slowly got to her feet. Although she was still pale, her mouth was firmly set.

'What do you want to meet her for?' Marco regarded her in open dismay.

'Are you scared of what I might find? So am I . . . but it would be much more scary to sit at home wondering,' she confided.

It was already the middle of the afternoon. It was over two hundred miles to the small village where Elissa lived but Sara climbed into the Jag with unassailable determination. Alex might well have gone by the time she arrived . . . well, so be it. It was Elissa whom Sara needed to meet. She did not want to see Alex with the wretched woman. Such an encounter required a certain discretion, didn't it?

The further north Sara got, the more tense she became. Suddenly she doubted her own sanity, the need to *know* which had blanked out every other prompting. Alex had kept his continuing acquaintance with Elissa a secret even from his family . . . for how many years? And how did she know that he only saw Elissa twice a year? Pete would only be aware of those visits when Alex went directly from the office. And Elissa was discreet, wasn't she? Pete had only *once* spoken to her on the phone. The perfect mistress . . . ?

She stopped for a meal at a motorway service station. She was exhausted and she forced herself to eat and drink simply to keep going. It was much later than she had hoped when she finally came upon the old stone farmhouse which lay about a mile outside the village on a steep, narrow road. There wasn't a single glimmer of life or light about Elissa's home. Sara stopped the car and rested her aching head back. So what now?

Was he in there with her? The idea totally wiped Sara out. Two long-time lovers entangled in the comfort of an adulterous bed . . . In silent agony she shut her eyes. Elissa had betrayed her first husband—why should she think twice about betraying a woman she had never even met? Why hadn't Alex married her? Why had she left him in the first place? Why hadn't he told Sara the truth?

But no, he hadn't lied except by omission. So what was the secret of Elissa's enduring appeal? If he still loved her, wouldn't he have married her?

And then finally Sara grasped wearily at an explanation for behaviour which struck her as incomprehensible. Only last night Alex had told her that he could understand a sexual obsession. Was that Elissa's continuing attraction after all these years? Was it possible that Alex had married her to try and break free of that affair? And was it possible that she had driven him straight back into Elissa's waiting arms again?

Sara hit her lowest ebb then. Alex *had* been happy with her. She wouldn't have had the courage to put her pride on the line today had she not been clinging to that awareness. Only Alex had not responded . . . Alex had been implacably cold and unimpressed.

Why had she come up here? What had she hoped to achieve by confronting a woman who probably knew Alex so much better than she did? Forcing herself on Elissa would be demeaning and pointless. It sunk in on Sara then that Alex really was gone, that it would be pathetic to pursue him one more step, that he had left her with nothing to do but retire in defeat. Her whole world fell in pieces around her the minute she reached that conclusion. She covered her convulsing face with her hands, a choked sob of despair ripped from her working throat.

Suddenly someone tapped on the windscreen and she was in such a state that she didn't even jump. She looked up and saw a woman in an incongruous pink dressing gown hovering. Gulping, she buzzed down the window a few inches.

'Sara?' the woman said uncertainly. 'You are Sara, aren't you? I looked out when I heard a car stop. Alex described this car to me. Would you like to come in?'

'In?' Sara echoed, blinking at the lights now illuminating the previously dark house.

'I'm going to look really daft if a car comes along,' the woman pointed out gently. 'And it's beginning to rain.'

'You're...Elissa?' The soft Scottish accent was equally disconcerting. Sara had simply assumed that Elissa was Italian.

'Everyone but Alex calls me Liz now.'

Sara snatched in a steadying breath and climbed out of the Jag, trying not to stare.

'I'm afraid you've missed him. I assume that's why you're here...but he hardly ever stays over. Still, I'm glad you came,' Elissa asserted, as if Sara's unannounced arrival were perfectly normal. 'I hate being on my own at night. John took the kids up to his mother's this evening and he won't be back until morning.'

'John?'

'My husband.' Elissa thrust wide the door of her home and Sara saw her properly for the first time.

She wasn't exactly seduction personified, in a pink towelling robe and fluffy mules. Not my double either, Sara registered, still staring. She had wide blue eyes, very curly, short dark brown hair and a figure that verged more on the plump than the petite. But she had a beautiful face and the sort of vivacious warmth that just leapt out and grabbed you.

Elissa was looking Sara over with equal fascination. 'I've been dying to meet you but Alex didn't think it was a good idea.'

'Didn't he?'

'He didn't say so.' Elissa grimaced, pushing open the door of a cosy, cluttered kitchen. 'Alex can be very tactful when he wants to be but I could see him bristling the way he does when you put your feet in it...which I always do around Alex. He's not at all like John. John is wonderfully easy to live with... *Sorry*!' Like a dismayed child who had dropped a brick, Elissa clapped a hand to her mouth.

'You don't need to apologise,' Sara assured her with a glimmer of slowly awakening amusement. 'Actually, I came up here thinking you were having an affair with Alex.'

Elissa frowned in astonishment. 'But why?'

'Alex had neglected to mention the fact that he was still in touch with you.'

'I did ask him not to tell anyone. I left my old life behind and I don't want it to catch up with me again. John knows all about it, of course, but I would hate Alex's family to know we're still in touch. They really hate me,' she sighed. 'But Alex has done so much for us since our first business went bankrupt. We couldn't have gotten through that without him. He helped us get back on our feet and then start up again. Good grief…an affair,' she repeated, as if Sara's words were only now sinking in.

She swept a pile of laundry off a chair while Sara studied a montage of photos on a pinboard. 'Your children?'

'Well, technically John's. He was a widower with three children under five when we met up ten years ago. A match made in heaven,' Elissa joked. 'This was my fresh start.' She hesitated. 'I got in touch with Alex a couple of years after we broke up because I still felt guilty. I mean, I just ran out on him, which was pretty hateful after the way he'd stood by me.'

'Why did you leave?' Sara murmured.

Elissa gave her a wry look. 'I was making a mess of his life, Sara. He wasn't happy with me. He wouldn't admit it but I could feel it. I owed him so much. Without Alex's support, I would never have had the courage to leave Sal… My first husband was a very violent man,' she said tautly. 'Alex felt sorry for me. I started depending on him and the rest you can probably guess.'

'Yes,' Sara said with sympathy. 'I'm sorry I landed on your doorstep like this—'

'But how brave when you thought what you did.' Elissa surveyed her with amused but frank admiration. 'My lack of guts always got on Alex's nerves.'

'Can I ask you why Alex came up here today?'

'He owns the majority of our business, Sara. We import terracotta from Italy,' Elissa explained cheerfully. 'He refinanced us when we couldn't get a loan after going bust the first time. John isn't terribly good with money and Alex keeps an eye on things. Well, to be honest, he watches us like a hawk so that we don't overextend ourselves again. He doesn't make much of a profit out of us either. He's been a very generous friend.'

Sara smothered an embarrassing yawn.

Elissa laughed. 'You can't possibly get back behind that wheel again. Will you stay the night?'

Alex hadn't even confided in Elissa, Sara thought as she drove back home by easy stages the next day. Elissa had thought that he was a little quiet, but had noticed nothing else apart from the fact that he'd appeared to be in a distinct hurry to leave again. 'A very generous friend', she had said. But was there something more on Alex's side? Was that why he had chosen not to tell her that he still saw the other woman? And what did it matter now anyway? she asked herself despondently as she turned up the drive to Ladymead. Nothing she had found out made the slightest difference really. Alex had left her. Yesterday his attitude to her had hardened even more. He had told her that he wanted a divorce.

In the frame of mind that she was in, it was a heck of a shock when the first thing she saw as she got out of her car was Alex striding towards her.

'*Dio*, where the hell have you been?' he demanded explosively. 'I've been up all night worrying myself sick. I was going to ring the police again!'

Sara blinked in bewilderment at this astonishing transformation. Her tongue cleaved to the roof of her dry mouth. Alex closed his arms round her with such force that he very nearly knocked her off her feet. 'It doesn't matter where you have been,' he groaned then, releasing his breath with unconcealed relief. 'You've come home.'

Wide-eyed, she gazed up at him, taking in the tousled hair, the heavy blue shadow of stubble on his usually clean-shaven jawline, the shadows beneath his feverish dark eyes. 'Alex—'

'Please don't ever do this to me again.' With an obvious effort he loosened a grip that was threatening to crack her ribs and grasped her hands tautly in his. 'I have now lived through the worst forty-eight hours of my life. I know I asked for it, but shout at me the next time, don't disappear! Not that there'll be a *next* time,' he hurried to assure her emphatically. 'I'll never take a risk like that with you again!'

Alex had come home. Alex was practically on his knees with gratitude that she had come home. Her head swam. Obviously he hadn't been in touch with Marco... Either that or Marco had decided to keep quiet. In a daze she looked at the glossy black head bent over their linked hands. 'We're not on the brink of a divorce any more?' she asked, just to check.

His head flew up, stark guilt and discomfiture clenching his vibrantly handsome features. 'I was sick with jealousy and bitterness, *cara*. I wanted to hit back and yet the whole time you were standing there I was cutting myself in two as well.'

'You were like the iceman,' Sara whispered reflectively with a shiver.

'I didn't want you to know how much you had hurt me,' he muttered gruffly.

'When did you come back?'

'Yesterday... as soon as I could. I assumed you'd be here... and then I called everywhere I could think of and panic set in. I was afraid you had had an accident. I checked with the police.'

'I went up north to meet Elissa.'

In the act of walking her into the house, Alex spun his dark head to her at speed. 'You... *what*?'

'I spent the night there. I liked her—'

'You spent the night?'

Sara relished his stunned reaction. 'When I heard that name, I thought I had discovered a secret mistress. I decided to confront her—'

'*Dio*...' Alex had paled. 'So that is where you have been all this time.'

'But I soon realised I had nothing to worry about. I don't know where anyone got the idea that Elissa and I look alike...'

'Sandro started that nonsense at the wedding,' Alex admitted grudgingly, his arm tightening round her as if he feared that she might pull away. 'Elissa once had long dark hair, but that was the only real similarity between you. Sandro has very poor eyesight but he's too vain to wear spectacles. I doubt if he even remembers Elissa that well.'

'Yet Claudia told me I was Elissa's double.'

Alex vented an angry imprecation in his own language.

Sara smiled sweetly. 'And I don't recall you denying it when I mentioned the idea. Do you think you could explain that, Alex?'

A slight darkening of colour had highlighted his hard cheekbones.

'Stuck for a ready excuse?' she probed in mock disbelief. 'I don't believe it.'

He released his breath in a hiss. 'I thought a little jealousy might give your thoughts a new direction—'

'Back to you... and away from Brian,' Sara guessed. 'But then I wasn't thinking about Brian at the time.'

'Every time I saw your face cloud, every time you went quiet, I assumed he was on your mind,' Alex confessed tautly. 'I couldn't stop doing it even though I realised I was being unreasonable. After all, I had married you knowing that you loved another man. I thought I could be patient but I found that a much tougher challenge than I had imagined.'

'You should have told me you were still in contact with Elissa.'

'My family have the very embarrassing habit of behaving as though Elissa was this great tragic love who wrecked my life and broke my heart and whom I never recovered from,' Alex said through decidedly gritted teeth. 'I didn't mind you wondering a little about that affair but I certainly didn't want you getting the same maudlin ideas fixed in your head.'

'Didn't you put them there in the first place?'

'The day I told you about her, I was attempting to empathise with you,' Alex admitted wryly. 'But I was very young when I met Elissa. It was first love and intense but I wasn't ready to make the kind of commitment she needed. She was right to leave before we ended up hating each other but at the time I felt she had just used me as an escape from a rotten marriage. Meeting up with her again a couple of years later put paid to that. We were both able to laugh about what a bad match we were once the romance wore off.'

'So you stayed friends?'

'No, we went our separate ways until three years ago when she phoned and asked me for financial advice. John had just been declared bankrupt. They were in a real mess. I was happy to help.'

'That was a kind thing to do.'

Alex shrugged. 'They're a pleasant couple, but hopeless in business.'

'Were you really worried sick about me last night?' Sara pressed.

'Panicking.' His deep voice fractured as his eyes collided with her searching gaze.

'So when did you decide to come home?'

'Five minutes after the helicopter took off.' Alex reached for her hands again. 'I know I was a real swine but I was hurting myself as much as I was hurting you. *Dio, cara*, I have loved you for so long...'

'How long?' she whispered shakily.

'The first month you started working for me,' Alex confided heavily.

In shock, Sara stared back at him. 'But you told me you didn't believe in love—'

'Sara, I would have told you the sky was pink if it would have impressed you. I would have done and said anything it took to persuade you that it was a good idea to marry me,' Alex admitted, scanning her shaken face with wry comprehension. 'If I had told you how I really felt, it might have frightened you off. You're so considerate about other people's feelings that you could have decided it wouldn't be fair to marry me.'

'So you offered me a marriage of convenience.'

'Non-threatening.'

'And didn't complain about anything until you had that ring on my finger,' Sara said, and she remembered him saying that he had expected too much from her and finally understood why. The knowledge that Alex had been in love with her for such a long time stunned her.

'I was terrified you would get cold feet.'

'But you smouldered in silence.'

'I thought I could be patient—'

'You're not the patient type,' she interposed absently.

'And when I heard that Brian and your cousin had split up and guessed where you had to be...' Alex paused, his dark eyes revealing lingering pain. 'And you'd lied to me. It was one hell of a shock. I went right off the rails—'

'Alex, I—' Sara began strickenly, distressed by what she read in his expressive gaze.

'But I still came back. I didn't believe your version of events for one moment, though. Then your aunt phoned this morning and asked me to tell you that she was grateful for a little favour you'd done for her and would I please pass on the message that Brian and Antonia were talking again. She had no idea that I knew what she was referring to...' Alex's troubled features clenched. 'Sara...I should have trusted you.'

'When people lie, trust can be very difficult,' she conceded softly.

'If you hadn't lied, you wouldn't have done any little favour,' Alex gritted. 'I'd have torn him limb from limb!'

'No, you might have felt sorry for him. Antonia faked being pregnant.'

Alex absorbed that with a complete lack of interest, his burning gaze engaged in roving over her. 'Did you mean it when you said you loved me?'

Sara lifted possessive hands to his broad shoulders and looked up at him with glowing eyes. 'What do you think?'

'I think I want you to say it at least once every five minutes.'

'I love you...'

His lean hands were unsteady as he cupped her cheeks. 'I don't know how you didn't *see* that I was madly in love with you, greedy for your attention, possessive of your every thought...'

His hungry mouth closed over hers and the aching emptiness was banished for ever as he hauled her up into his arms and carried her upstairs. 'Would you really have to be a mental case to want my baby?' he muttered between hot, drugging kisses that made her wildly responsive senses swim.

'Do we get to do this a lot in pursuit of the objective?'

'Do we need an excuse?'

They decided that they didn't and concentrated on the difficulties of getting undressed when neither of them was prepared to stop long enough to accomplish that feat. A long time later they lay entwined, so mutually entranced that even the sound of a not too distant workman's hammer didn't penetrate the heady sense of wonder they were both experiencing.

And then a stray thought occurred to Sara. 'Alex...do you think you could fix Brian up with a better job?'

As his dark eyes shimmered and tensed Sara rested a teasing fingertip against the compressed line of his mouth. 'I don't object to you helping Elissa and her family, do I?'

'No, but—'

'Brian and Antonia's marriage would have a much better chance of succeeding if he was earning a bit more.'

His tension evaporated as that sank in.

Sara smiled with sunny satisfaction at him. 'I'm learning how to think like you do, my love—you had better watch out.'

'All that jealousy stuff is behind me,' Alex asserted, fiercely on the defensive.

'Because now you know you didn't need to be jealous. I started falling for you the very first day; how could I have failed to do anything else?' Sara leant over him, tenderly amused that Alex could have his insecurities too. 'You're gorgeous, you're sexy, and sneaky only when it's in my best interests...and, by the way, Brian does not want to work in Alaska.'

'Dubai...currently doing very well in the tourist market? They would get a break from an interfering bunch of in-laws, a lively social life, sunshine and a maid to do the cooking.' Alex treated her to a slashing smile of megawatt intensity. 'What do you think?'

'I think you're going to keep me on my toes,' Sara admitted, transfixed by the speed with which he had responded to the challenge.

'And *I* think that you are the best thing that ever happened to me, *bella mia*.' And with the aid of one passionate kiss Alex ensured that other people's problems were the very last thing on her mind. She gave herself up blissfully to sensation instead.

HARLEQUIN PRESENTS®

PENNY JORDAN

"Penny Jordan pens a formidable read."
—*Romantic Times*

Harlequin brings you the best books by the best authors!

Watch for:
#1839 THE TRUSTING GAME

Christa had learned the hard way that men were not to be trusted. So why should she believe Daniel when he said he could teach her to trust?

Harlequin Presents—the best has just gotten better!
Available in October wherever
Harlequin books are sold.

TAUTH-13

HARLEQUIN PRESENTS®

For your eyes only!

Dear Reader,

re: SWEET SINNER by Diana Hamilton
   Harlequin Presents #1841

Zoe's boss, James, had formed the worst
possible impression of Zoe and branded her a
heartless tramp. Could she ever convince him
that he was *so* wrong?

Yours sincerely,

The Editor at Harlequin Mills & Boon

P.S. Harlequin Presents—the best has just
      gotten better! Available in October
      wherever Harlequin books are sold.

P.P.S. Look us up on-line at: http://www.romance.net

NINE4

Sabrina   It Happened One Night
Working Girl   Pretty Woman
While You Were Sleeping

If you adore romantic comedies then have
we got the books for you!

Look for Harlequin's
LOVE & LAUGHTER™
at your favorite retail outlet. It's a brand-new
series with two books every month capturing
the lighter side of love.

You'll enjoy humorous love stories by favorite
authors and brand-new writers, including
JoAnn Ross, Lori Copeland, Jennifer Crusie,
Kasey Michaels and many more!

As an added bonus—with the purchase, at
retail, of two new Love & Laughter books you
can receive a **free** copy of our fabulous
Love and Laughter collector's edition.

LOVE & LAUGHTER™—a natural
combination...always
romantic...always entertaining

HARLEQUIN ®